THE

GENERAL'S

BEARD

Modern Fiction from Korea
published by Homa & Sekey Books

Father and Son: A Novel by Han Sung-won

Reflections on a Mask: Two Novellas by Ch'oe In-hun

Unspoken Voices: Selected Short Stories by Korean Women Writers by Park Kyong-ni et al.

The General's Beard: Two Novellas by Lee Oyoung

Farmers: A Novel by Lee Mu-young

THE GENERAL'S

BEARD

TWO NOVELLAS

Lee Oyoung

Translated from the Korean by

Brother Anthony of Taizé

Homa & Sekey Books

Dumont, New Jersey

The publication of this book was supported by a grant from
Korea Literature Translation Institute.

ISBN: 1-931907-07-2
Library of Congress Control Number: 2002103288

Publishers Cataloging-in-Publication Data

The General's Beard: Two Novellas by Lee, Oyoung, 1934-
Translated from the Korean by Brother Anthony of Taizé
1. Korean fiction--20th century--Translation into English
2. Korean fiction--Translations into English
3. English fiction--Translations from the Korean
I. Title. PL992.62 895.734-dc21

Published by Homa & Sekey Books
138 Veterans Plaza
P. O. Box 103
Dumont, NJ 07628

Tel: (201)384-6692
Fax: (201)384-6055
Email: info@homabooks.com
Website: www.homabooks.com

Editor-in-chief: Shawn X. Ye
Executive Editor: Judy Campbell

Printed in the United States of America
1 3 5 7 9 10 8 6 4 2

Contents

Translator's Note

Born in 1934, Lee Oyoung graduated from the Humanities College of Seoul National University and completed an M.A. there before embarking on his remarkable career. He became a professor in the Humanities College at Ewha Women's University in Seoul in 1966. At the same time, beginning in 1960, he began to serve as an editorialist with a number of major daily newspapers. He is a polymath of international stature, perhaps best known abroad for his role in planning the opening and closing ceremonies of the 1988 Seoul Olympic Games. In 1990, he was appointed to be the Republic of Korea's first Minister of Culture, a position he held until 1991. After that he headed a variety of major government and presidential committees, including one responsible for the commemoration of the 50th Anniversary of Korean Independence in 1995, and another in preparation for the new Millennium. He returned to Ewha Women's University as Chair Professor for a number of years, before becoming Standing Advisor to the *Chungang Ilbo* daily newspaper in 2001.

In the 1960s, he wrote a small number of works of short fiction, including the novellas *The General's Beard* (1967) and *Phantom Legs* (1969) as well as a collection of short stories, *Wartime Decameron*. After that, Lee Oyoung virtually abandoned literary writing until the publication in 1993 of a novel which received considerable critical acclaim. Lee Oyoung is widely known in Korea for his articles, essays and critical writings, covering a vast range of topics: artistic, literary, social, philosophical, cultural, and political. One of his main concerns has always been to explore the interaction of different cultures in the modern age and to promote the reception of traditional Korean culture in today's globalized world. His study of modern

Japan, first written in Japanese and published in English as *Smaller is Better*, is recognized in the realm of Japanese studies as the classic study of Japanese culture.

In writing *The General's Beard*, Lee Oyoung set out to explore the uncertainties inherent in any attempt to account in a narrative for another person's actions. *The General's Beard* is a detective story that is made complex by the presence within it of quotations from the journal of the young man, Ch'ol-Hun, whose mysterious death forms the starting-point of the story. The main narrator sets out to try to discover how and why Ch'ol-Hun died. Much of what he discovers derives from the journal he left behind but he is also able to meet a young girl, Shin-Hyei, with whom he had had a brief liaison. She provides other elements of information but their relationship failed and they had broken up before Ch'ol-Hun's death. What we gradually sense is Ch'ol-Hun's despair in the face of the conflict between a dream of innocence and purity and the demands of existence in an absurd and brutal society. Part of the conflicts explored in the story stem from the brutal passage from traditional rural life to modern industrialized society in recent Korean history.

Ironically, the title of Lee Oyoung's novella, *The General's Beard*, is the title of a novel that Ch'ol-Hun had been trying to write, which is mentioned briefly, quoted, and summarized during the tale, but which Ch'ol-Hun had left unfinished at his death. The novella offers no complete solutions to the puzzle of why Ch'ol-Hun decided to end his own life, no closure to any of the unfinished narratives. This makes Lee Oyoung's work a remarkably sophisticated piece of avant-garde, post-modern literature.

The second work, *Phantom Legs*, explores the relations between literary fiction and real life in another way by intercalating long extracts from Stendhal's *Vanina Vanini* into a young Korean girl's recollections of her relationship with a young student activist she first met during the dramatic events of April 19, 1960, when the Korean army opened fire on groups of students protesting against the political corruption of the Syngman Rhee regime. In May 1961, the Korean military staged a coup and radical social protest was driven underground. The story explores the contrast between the romantic tale of the early 19-century Italian countess and the outlaw she falls in love with in Stendhal's work and the much less satisfactory story of Sa-Mi's uncertain relationship with the student activist Chon Hyon-Su. The pain she feels is set in parallel with that experienced by amputees, who suffer agonies in "phantom" limbs that are no longer there.

Finally, I gratefully acknowledge the support I received from the Korean Culture and Arts Foundation in translating this work.

Brother Anthony of Taizé
Seoul
March, 2002

The General's Beard

1

"Is this some kind of interrogation?"

I rose abruptly from the sofa where I had been sitting. I kept my voice low. His name card fluttered from the table but he did not pick it up. I reckoned it was good to show some open signs of ill humor. It was too humiliating just to sit there like a criminal, meekly answering his questions. One of the buttons on Inspector Park's homespun waistcoat was swinging to and fro, hanging by a thread. Was that what had irritated me?

Detective Inspector Park also rose. He seemed about to grab me by the lapels. I pretended not to notice, turned my back on him, and walked toward the window. It was only a little after one o'clock, yet it was already growing dark in the hotel room. Perhaps it was snowing outside? As I raised the window blind, I spoke again, rather more boldly and harshly.

"I've already told you, I have absolutely no memory of his name. I have already repeated it at least three times in exactly the same words. He presented himself as a reporter from the photo section of some newspaper; that was all I knew of him. I only ever met him once. As I said, we just had a drink together. I can't even remember the name of the bar now. I met him at the introduction of someone called Kim in the photo section, so wouldn't it be simpler if you paid him a visit? If you keep saying, 'That's impossible,' like that, aren't you inviting me to tell lies? What's all this about, anyway?"

The simple fact of a stranger coming to pay me a visit here in this hotel was in itself no pleasure. Even if he had brought a

13

bottle of Frontera sherry with him, I would not have been very pleased. No one was supposed to know that I was staying at the Savannah Hotel. No one except the publishing house that had sent me there. So this detective had not come to visit me simply because he happened to have my address, like a postman. He must have traced my whereabouts with the help of several assistants, like a criminal, a wanted criminal. It was obvious that once having put himself to the trouble of coming all the way out to this hotel, he was not about to turn tail and take his leave with a bow and a scrape. Which meant...well, which meant that this detective must be laboring under some enormous misapprehension.

Inspector Park walked across to the window where I was standing. Then as I stared out, he spoke from behind me as if he were reading from a document. I found his voice, devoid of all intonation and emotion, oddly irritating.

"He's dead. The day before yesterday. The first day it snowed. Kim Ch'ol-Hun died some time during the night. Only..."

"Only what? Have you been asked to bring me some inheritance? What connection are you suggesting exists between me and his death, for goodness sake? This is no undertaker's shop. Neither is it a very suitable place in which to discuss the death of someone with whom I am quite unrelated. I'm sorry, but can't you just go away? The publishers will be none too pleased if they hear how you're taking up my time like this. After all, they're the ones paying for this room. These hours don't belong to me, you know."

Learning that he was dead merely seemed to make me more nervous. Only now a strange feeling of apprehension was beginning to make itself felt too. I sensed that my fingers that had been holding a cigarette since the moment I first met Inspector Park's gaze were trembling slightly.

The sky was clouding over but it had not begun to snow yet. In that expanse of gray pollution, the November city spread, freezing. Old buildings lay slumped on the asphalt like rats in a trap. Nothing had changed since yesterday. Nothing was changing at all. There was nothing at all to make me nervous. So why was I standing there like that, angry and fretful and feeling so apprehensive? What was the reason for it? Surely that man's death, no matter how it came about, had nothing to do with me.

Inspector Park remained unruffled even when I told him to go away. Rather he smiled, as if we were friends talking.

"Of course, I have this kind of job but I'm a great admirer of your novels; I've read them all without skipping a line. From the very outset I had no intention of interrogating you. Only you must collaborate with us. We don't mean to trouble people, but we're determined to find out why he died."

Inspector Park pulled out his lighter and applied the flame to the cigarette I was holding in my mouth. It was only then that I realized it had gone out. His voice reached me across a great distance, as if it were coming from behind the wall, in the next room.

Ch'ol-Hun was dead. It had happened on the same day that his mother came up to Seoul from the village where she lived. It was his mother who had discovered the body. The room was full of the stink of coal fumes. Strangely enough, the lid of the coal-briquette stove was off. Ch'ol-Hun was lying sprawled on the floor with his hands clasped, like someone praying.

"He died of carbon monoxide poisoning. Only it was no simple accident caused by negligence. It was either suicide or murder. After all, he was a press photographer. He had easier methods available if he wanted to kill himself. He regularly handled poisons when he was developing his films. Besides, he

15

was fond of his mother. Even if he meant to kill himself, surely he would have wanted to meet his mother first. Yet it happened in the night prior to the very day his mother was due to arrive."

We returned to the sofa and sat down.

"It was the first time I've ever seen a suicide who didn't cut his finger nails first. It's really quite fascinating. Not a single suicide is capable of making a complete break with the world. Even when they've got fed up with living and are doing away with themselves, they still worry about afterward. For instance, they take care not to make any mistakes in writing the suicide note, or they take a bath and put on clean clothes before dying so that their corpse won't look grubby. They can never stop worrying about what people will think. There are even some, the really bad cases, who go so far as to offer the press articles so as to dramatize their suicide. The contents are always grossly exaggerated. It's astonishing the number of pessimists there are in this world who die wondering just how many articles their suicide will provoke. I've dealt with any number of suicides and one point they all had in common was an inability to uproot completely every last trace of lingering attachment to life, and the way they all arranged to leave behind some melodramatic kind of testimony in their preparations for death. That's what's bothering me. The fact that in the case of Kim Ch'ol-Hun there is not one trace of any of those characteristic signs of a suicide. If it really was a suicide, it's the most absolute and perfect suicide anyone was ever capable of committing. Only I believe no one can kill themselves like that."

"You mean it was homicide? And if homicide...."

Now I was questioning him, in nervous tones.

"That is precisely the problem. Whatever bruises there were, he got them falling from the bed. I'm still waiting for the autopsy report, but there's no doubt about its being carbon monoxide poisoning. It might be assumed that someone waited until he was asleep, then took the lid off his coal-briquette stove. Only there's no sign of anything having been touched. More important still is the fact that he seems not to have had a single close friend. Even at work, he's reported almost never to have associated with his colleagues. He had nothing worth stealing, let alone worth killing for. There are only two things that look suspicious: one is that his camera couldn't be found, the other is the fact that the previous week he and the woman he'd been living with for six months broke up. His camera was a Rollei-Code, but after he quit the newspaper job he was unemployed for a long time. Don't you think a musician, say, if he's destitute, will sell the instrument that was like his own flesh and blood to him, in order to buy some food? We can't assume for certain that someone stole that camera. I met the woman too. Her alibi was waterproof and there was nothing dirty hidden in her relationship with him. It wouldn't be bad as the subject for a novel, I reckon. Don't you agree?"

Inspector Park seemed to be setting a trap for me. I felt obliged to make some kind of reply.

"You mean you want me to write a novel. Now you're not interrogating me, but giving me a lecture about creative writing, I suppose? You'd better bring a better subject next time."

Inspector Park assumed a solemn air once again and drew a crumpled envelope from the same inside pocket from which he had previously produced his name card.

"But fortunately there's still one last clue left: this letter. We found this letter that he must have written just a few hours before he died. You hold the last key to this incident. So please help us."

"A suicide note? That's not what you were saying just now. You must be happy that he left a sign of suicide like other people, after all."

I had the feeling that Inspector Park was playing with me.

It was no suicide note, however. It was a letter destined to be sent to me by way of the newspaper. It had my name clearly written on the envelope. It even had stamps on but they had not been franked. The sender's name was there: Kim Ch'ol-Hun. My fingers began to tremble again. The letter was written on a page of college note paper, without any initial greeting, a few words scrawled like a memo:

When I see you next time, I'll show it to you finished. I can have it done in less than a week. I feel confident. I don't care if you smile. If it doesn't work, it's the end of me. I'm not even thinking about what might happen afterward. Could you let me have your address, please?

December 14.   Hun

Inspector Park opened his notebook.

"More like a telegram than a letter, isn't it? You must tell us what he means by 'it.' You told us you couldn't even recall his name, yet you're the person he destined to receive his last written words. Now we..."

At last I could laugh.

"All right. We've come by a very roundabout way. It's as though we'd left the nearest shortcut and gone wandering off somewhere. An indirect interrogation is sometimes the least scientific. Why didn't you show me this note to start with? Only I don't think you'll find it a particularly good clue. This 'it' refers to *The General's Beard*, you see. He..."

For the first time Inspector Park's face grew flushed.

"Please don't joke. I don't think they'd be very pleased down at the station if they thought I was sitting here listening dumbly to your jokes like this. This time doesn't belong to me, either. Suppose we save the jokes for outside of working hours, for when we're in a bar or something?"

He spoke as if he assumed that I had merely been joking. But my words had been the exact truth. The first time we had met at Kim's introduction, it had also been on account of *The General's Beard*.

He had wanted to write a novel. Only before he started to write, he wanted to discuss it with a novelist. In those days I was having a novel serialized in the newspaper he used to work for. Perhaps that was why he had chosen me.

The first time I set eyes on Kim Ch'ol-Hun, I did not think much of him. He looked like the kind of young man you can meet anywhere if you stand for just five minutes at the roadside.

Even now, except for the scar on his forehead, I cannot picture him at all. He was an ordinary youth, just one run-of-the-mill young man.

He was one of those fellows who worries all the time about getting failing grades at school yet has nothing brilliant but his dreams; there he becomes a public official with his own secretary, happens to fall in love with a millionaire's beautiful daughter (his only child, if possible), goes abroad to study, gets a Ph.D. in the States, rides about in a Cadillac, hangs out with diplomats, plays bridge with them...then stuffing all those dreams into his rucksack, he goes off to the wars, buries the fragments of his shattered dreams among exploding mortars and smoke shells, then goes about grumbling that society has nothing much to be said for it, but he'd like to get himself a well-paid job. He was one of those aspiring fellows who, when this and that and everything turns boring, goes about saying how everyone wants at least once to write some kind of novel.

If there was anything particular in his case, it was simply the fact that the title of the novel he was planning to write one day was an odd one: *The General's Beard*. As for the plot, it was somewhat absurd, just about what might be expected from an admirer of Kafka.

As soon as the alcohol took hold of him, Ch'ol-Hun became garrulous. Originally he had said that he needed to learn a lot from me, but it turned out quite differently and he went on and on in a hostile tirade.

Despite the nervous glances of Kim, who was sitting beside him, Ch'ol-Hun kept affirming excitedly that the modern Korean novel was too anemic and that writers were mere bakers, incapable of anything except sprinkling yeast on newspaper articles to make them swell up.

I just sat staring at the "no credit" sign fixed to the bar wall and smiled, now at the odd etymology of the word credit, a combination of the Chinese characters "out" and "over," and now at the two characters for "no," one a so polite "thanks" and the other a warlike "cut off," the two hobbling along like a cripple, as I listened to what he said. That was the sum total of all that had passed between us.

"Really? Then the letter means that he was going to write a novel. Do you..."

Inspector Park nodded in the direction of the wall that was papered with a hempen weave. His face reminded me of a punctured balloon.

"I wonder if you can recall the broad outlines of the plot of the novel he mentioned that day? It probably won't be of much help but there were sheets of note paper spread across his desk. He had obviously been writing something...."

"I don't see that the novel could have contained anything worth killing him for. Really, of course, what you might term a story is like a human skeleton. If that's all you've got, there's no way you can tell if the woman was pretty or ugly. That's what I told him: that a novel isn't something you talk about; it's something you write."

"Still, the novel's title was *The General's Beard*?"

THE GENERAL'S BEARD

I had the impression that Inspector Park was someone who hated wasting time and on account of that found himself wasting more time than ever.

"He said that his novel began on the morning of a day when there was a coup d'état. The main character was a low ranking employee in some office, but I'm not sure what his job was. Then there were the unshaven faces of the troops making the coup: they had been living for a long time hidden up in the hills, with no way of shaving....so down they all came with their long side-whiskers and beards. The only thing people could talk about that day was 'the general's beard,' that general who led the parade of rebel troops, and not at all why the coup had come about or what the nation's future would be like. You see, he had a beard just like all the others, but his was neatly trimmed and shaped. And he looked much smarter than the rest. Shall I go on?"

Inspector Park continued to stare at the patterned wallpaper. Outside it had started to snow. Freed now of my insecurity, I suddenly became talkative. I even felt sorry about my previous bad behavior. So I went on telling him about *The General's Beard*.

After the Revolution, people all began to grow beards just like "the general's beard." The civilians entering the revolutionary administration, in their struggles for power, began attacking one another over the growth of their beards.

Overnight, beards became a kind of symbol of a person's support for the Revolution. Not only the high grade civil servants, but the heads of government-run industrial firms, industrialists that had received favors, and bank managers, all began to turn up at public functions sporting beards just like the general's in token of their loyalty.

"The general's beard" spread like an epidemic. Everybody, from university presidents to rickshaw boys, grew beards and went parading through the streets. Every morning when people got up, their beards had grown a little longer, and the "general's beards" that had by now become standard in their immediate neighborhood increased one by one.

The point soon came where it was hard to live in society without a beard. The novel's hero, the office employee, began to feel increasingly uncomfortable. All around him, faces without beards began to disappear completely. If he entered a barber's shop, the barber would refuse to go anywhere near his beard with a razor blade. He was obliged to argue with the barber every time he went to have a haircut, and found himself quarrelling with people wearing beards. In buses and in restaurants, as well as in the street, he lived in a state of constant anxiety and fear under the stares of individuals regarding him out of the corner of their eyes, the stares of individuals with beards. But he refused to the bitter end to grow a "general's beard."

"If you feel uncomfortable, you only have to grow a beard too, don't you?"

That was all the advice his companions at work offered, each with a splendid beard that transformed their faces so that they had all turned into strangers.

The more uncomfortable he felt, the more firmly he refused to grow a beard. Yet soon even the few friends he had been trusting most began to appear with unshaven faces.

"Surely not? They've simply not shaved today."

All the same, as the days passed the area of beard would become more clearly pronounced. By the end of a month a completely different face would appear, as he had feared. People were gradually abandoning him.

THE GENERAL'S BEARD

His anxiety began to hinder him more and more severely. One day his boss, complete with a full-grown beard, summoned him. He found himself being urged to take a rest and get treatment.

He ventured to enquire: "Is it on account of the beard? Have they brought out a law making beards compulsory?"

His boss laughed behind his "general's beard." Then he scolded him in polite terms: this was a democracy where individual freedom was guaranteed by the constitution, so how could he possibly talk like that? It was precisely to cure him of that kind of obsession that he needed psychological treatment. Being labeled insane and getting driven from his job was by no means the end of his torments.

If he met people in the street and tried to ask something, all the beards seemed to flee from him. Then at night the beards would come to take their revenge. He had recurrent nightmares in which long beards wrapped themselves round him until he could no longer breathe. No matter where he went, thickets of beards pursued him, clutching at his neck as he tried to escape. He would wake from the dream as he hung writhing in the beards like a butterfly caught in a spider's web.

He tried surrendering to the authorities. He would get himself dead drunk, then kick open the police station door and go barging in. Going up to the officer in charge, with his "general's beard" he would beg him in tears: "Arrest me. I won't grow a beard, never. I won't. Put the handcuffs on quickly, and take me off to prison." But they only drove him out of the station. Growing a beard or not growing a beard was entirely up to each person's free choice. He found himself being dragged out by the constables on duty, each with his "general's beard." and dumped like trash at the curbside.

"He was dumped by the roadside, you say?" Inspector Park's eyes were shining. "A political novel? Was the 'general's beard' a term for our present government?"

I had the feeling that this was the first time I had heard Inspector Park ask anything with so much attention.

"A fable. A modern Aesop's fable. I suspect that Ch'ol-Hun intended to symbolize contemporary conformism by 'the general's beard.' He probably didn't mean to satirize any one particular period or the events in any particular country. You can say it was about the days of the kings of the Golden Age, about the days of Alexander the Great, or about an emperor that we cannot even imagine who will rule some day in the far distant future."

I was afraid that Inspector Park was getting the whole picture wrong again.

"...rule in the far distant future..."

Inspector Park kept repeating what I said, as if fascinated by something.

"Why yes. With every day that passes, society is become more intensely conformist. Only look at our shoes, our clothing, our pens, dishes, buttons, houses...everything is becoming more and more stereotyped. He wanted to deal with the way human destiny is going, the way everything, be it politics or daily ways of living, everything, our entire civilization, is being choked by that 'general's beard.' Only it was too intellectual for a novel, I would say...too intellectual a topic to succeed easily."

Inspector Park stared at the clock. The outside world was being buried under the first real snow of winter that was falling thickly. I saw Inspector Park out. Just as I opened the door I added a few last words to console him.

"It's a tricky assignment you've got. By the way, have you ever heard this story? It happened somewhere abroad. A young fellow was cleaning his revolver when it accidentally went off, fatally wounding him. As he was dying he managed to write on the wall: 'It was an accident,' so that people would know how he had died. Now I can understand why he acted that way. It's wrong to give investigators a lot of trouble. What do you say, wasn't it a suicide after all?"

I shook hands with Inspector Park. His grasp was weak.

"No. It must be murder. I'll have to find that missing camera. If you say it was suicide, you'll have to explain why, what reason there was for him to die. That's more a task for someone like you, a writer, a psychologist, a philosopher, than for me. If you agree, I could let you have a look at his note-books we've kept as evidence. And you could read his final text, too. It's at his home. His mother from the country is still staying there. If it appeals to you, that is."

I felt fatigue overwhelm me. Nothing was going to get written now. I fell onto the bed. The sound of Inspector Park's footsteps as he went down the stairs was absorbed into the gray space outside, where snow was falling. Then all was still. Why had that man died?

2

I passed through a number of dark, narrow, muddy alleys full of burned-out coal briquettes, scraps of egg-shell, the dried and twisted bodies of dead rats, all kinds of rubbish. Once past those alleys with their rows of collapsing wooden fences, I turned another corner. At the entry of the road I found myself in, a few women were peering into an alleyway and furtively muttering among themselves. As I turned into that same alley, they parted as if taken by surprise, casting anxious sideways glances at my face.

The house where Kim Ch'ol-Hun had rented a room stood at the very end of the alley, blocking it. It had probably originally been built by the Japanese to house railway officials. It was one of those old long wooden houses on two floors, now divided among a number of families and remodeled with a fence and gateway closing off each section. The whole building looked like a complicated maze. I checked once more the address from the back of the envelope that Inspector Park had left behind and at last located Kim Ch'ol-Hun's room.

The staircase leading up to the second floor was a prolongation of the dark alley outside, slippery and sordid, with the dead and rotting bodies of rats. Each step in the worn wooden stairway groaned wearily as I trod on it on my way up. The old sliding door in Japanese style, its fretwork covered with white paper, was rattling so noisily in the wind that there was no point in knocking. This was the room he had rented. I was taken aback on opening the door. On the bed at the other side of the room was sitting an old woman wearing a winter bonnet, her eyes closed in meditation like a Buddhist saint. At her feet, as if attending worship in a temple, I could see the back of a young woman with her head resting against the side of the bed. This was the room where Kim Ch'ol-Hun had died. Yet at the sight of them I found myself taken with a strong urge to laugh that I had to struggle to control. Because of the way I had been reminded of a temple.

The old woman slowly opened her eyes. As soon as she saw a new face, tears came flooding into her eyes. Yet the wrinkles embedded in her cheeks gave her a smiling air. She began to speak in soft and hoarse tones, as if talking to herself, but gradually her voice trembled louder.

"It's not right, not right. Give me back my boy right away. You mustn't cut him open; it's not right. You think I killed him.... But why? That I made him suffer like that because while he was alive he had that scar on his brow? It's not right to think such things. I tell you, it's not right if someone goes sticking a knife into my boy's body. Even if he's dead; you'll only add to his mother's heartache."

The old woman calmed down again and closed her eyes. A Buddhist rosary was wrapped round her hand.

She seemed to have taken me for someone from the police. Meanwhile the young woman introduced herself as Ch'ol-Hun's sister and drew up a chair for me. Then she began to whisper.

"Mother means that it would be wrong to perform a post-mortem. Why not? She is all the more upset because of a strange kind of guilty conscience."

"A guilty conscience?"

I spoke out loudly at the unexpected words. The old woman blinked her eyes open for a moment, then began to recite words from the Scriptures while counting her beads.

"Mother is convinced that he was killed because of that scar on his forehead. It happened when he was still just a nursing baby. She was sewing late one evening. My father's old grandmother was living in the house, which made life with her in-laws worse than usual, even at her age. She was nursing her baby and ironing at the same time, but finally fatigue overcame her and she fell asleep. Then something dreadful happened. In her sleep, her iron slipped...on the baby's forehead..."

"Her iron?…on his forehead?"

I recalled the scar branded vividly into his brow. Branded! I had simply assumed it was a wound he had got during the war. The old woman must still be marked with the scar of that burn too. That was why she was trying to prevent people from inflicting any more wounds on her dead son's body now.

"He never had any friends, not even as a child. He was always on his own. He used to spend hours shut up alone in the back room. Often we didn't even know he was there and would eat supper without him. Mother was always worrying that his character was warped like that on account of the brand on his forehead."

Suddenly the crazed old woman emitted a wail.

"No! No! Give me my boy back right now!"

I went toward the bed. There I paused for a moment, unsure of how I should address her. "Mother" "Missus" "Granny" I tried each of the words on my tongue. At last, although it felt indecent, I called her "Mother." I told her that I wasn't from the police, and that I had been Ch'ol-Hun's friend.

"Friend? You say his friend?"

Her response struck me as being exactly the opposite of Inspector Park's.

She was shaking her head slowly from side to side, as if to say, "You are someone completely unrelated with my son."

I too felt perplexed at having called him my "friend." Had I not reacted strongly when Inspector Park simply asked me if I knew Kim Ch'ol-Hun?

Why had I denied him so violently? Yet it was true. I really had been unable to recall Kim Ch'ol-Hun's name. But there was nothing base about it.

Not at all. Peter denied Jesus three times although he knew him very well. Surely it is only natural to deny when someone asks you if you know a complete stranger. Yet here I was now firmly calling him my friend. To put on a straight face and quite unnecessarily deny all knowledge of someone you can call your friend, that is base.

Given that we only met once and that he was someone whose name I could not recall, could I still really say that he meant nothing to me? In that case what had brought me to this place? Why was I so curious about his death? Why was I resolved to find out the reason he had died for? Was it to obtain material for a novel, as Inspector Park said? I was perplexed at the changes that had taken place, the way I called that old woman "mother" without the least embarrassment although it was the first time I set my eyes on her, or the way I calmly gave the name of "friend" to the very Kim Ch'ol-Hun that I had stoutly denied knowing to Inspector Park only the night before.

"Don't be offended; Mother's thinking of Ch'ol-Hun. There's only the two of us left now; mother is out of her mind. I used to lament having become a widow so young, but perhaps it was all for the best, seeing what's happened. It's hard for Mother."

I took care not to loose sight of my basic intention. I had come here to find out the cause of his death.

"Did Ch'ol-Hun really kill himself because of that scar? Other children used to make fun of it; then when he grew bigger he used to avoid company on account of it...that warped his personality...but he survived well enough until now, didn't he?"

The young woman adjusted the collar and fastenings of her dress. Can it be that people plunged in grief are not afraid of what others may think? The ribbons closing her dress had been hanging loose.

"Did Ch'ol-Hun never talk to you about his elder brother? If he killed himself, it might have been because of him. After what happened he never went so far as to mention his brother once. It's true that his scar isolated him from people, but having his brother taken from him like that was even more of a shock."

"Did he die?"

"He died in prison. Ch'ol-Hun was exceptionally fond of his brother, perhaps because he could never make any other friends; that brother was his only playmate. It was only after Liberation in 1945 that we found out he'd joined the Reds; it had been a mistake to send him to study in Japan. As soon as Liberation came, he kept on at Father about how he ought to redistribute his land to the landless peasants. It was awful. He used to get hold of Ch'ol-Hun too and tell him all sorts of strange things, though he was still only in primary school. In the end they were not allowed to meet inside the house at all. He got the kids of the tenant farmers together and set up a party cell. That got him kicked out of the house. Father threw him out."

The old woman was still counting her beads. The black grains of the rosary slipped noiselessly between her fingers that were thin as bamboo leaves.

"That must have affected him a lot."

I tried to get her to agree with me, but she paid no attention. Instead she continued in a kind of soliloquy.

"That happened much later. It was the evening; the rats had been skittering and slithering about up in the ceiling all day long. It was raining and the wind was blowing. After two years' absence, his brother came rushing into the house, soaked to the skin. He stood there shivering like an animal and scattering drops of rain. He begged us to hide him, and at the same time he kept railing at someone. 'It's all his fault I'm going to die,' he said. He went raving on about how he wasn't a Red now, or anything like it, or anything at all. Even now, we don't know what had happened, although maybe Ch'ol-Hun knew. He had come back home for the vacation just then; he was already more or less grown up. Besides, he was the only one his brother talked to at all."

"So did your father forgive him?"

I was curious about what had occurred. "Father..." she repeated after me.

His father no sooner set eyes on him than he dragged him outside. The older brother had knelt there on the ground in the pouring rain, pleading, but his father had not forgiven him.

"I can forgive you. But our ancestors will never forgive you."

With those words he ordered him to leave. Ch'ol-Hun had knelt beside his brother in the rain, imploring. He pointed out that they had lost all their ancestors' land in the reforms, so he should forgive his brother. That really put their father's back up. As soon as he heard the words 'land reform' he went mad. It was because there were people with their kind of ideas that the land reform had happened, he said. It was all the fault of louts like them, if he could no longer wield a sickle before his ancestors, and if the world had changed so much.

Then the police who had been pursuing him came and dragged him away.

"It was dreadful," the woman added. "After that, Ch'ol-Hun fell sick. Whenever it rained, he used to leap out of bed and go rushing out, saying that his brother was calling him. It was frightening, dreadful."

"I suppose his brother must have called out to Ch'ol-Hun as he was being carried off?"

"He kept calling him. He said he had something to tell him; he tried to get near him. He said he was sorry about something, too. He was carted off, all the time shouting, while Ch'ol-Hun couldn't follow after him or weep for him. It was as if his lips were sealed and his ears stopped up. That night he developed a fever and grew scalding hot, as hot as a cauldron on a fire, that sick he was. He clenched his lips together so hard that they had bruises on them. I never saw Ch'ol-Hun cry after that. When Father died, he only wailed for him once."

"Mother...you ought to get some rest."

That was the word I used, exactly like a son addressing his mother, as I seized the hands of the old woman sitting there on the bed. I had grown close to Ch'ol-Hun now he was dead.

It had been a six-tatami room. The mats had been stripped from off its wooden floor, but it felt even larger, maybe because of the lack of furnishings. There was no fire in the coal-briquette stove. Some pictures were hanging on the wall above the writing-table. There was one, by Géricault I think, showing a tilting raft full of shipwrecked people, some of them gesturing toward the horizon. Amidst the storm and darkness, they are waving their clothes in a plea for help.

A writing-table and some bookshelves, a desk-lamp, a cabinet, and a cracked vase...there was one large window opening westward, which looked as though sunlight would only penetrate there just before sunset. The room was remarkably like a cavern.

"Don't let them cut him open. Don't let them wound him. You mustn't forget my merits."

The old woman started to cry, recalling the violence that would be done to the corpse during the autopsy. I promised that I would talk to Inspector Park about it, although with no great conviction.

Finally, rummaging in his bookshelves, I was able to lay my hands on a number of his notebooks. Although the police had taken various things away, part of his diary had been left behind.

I took my leave of the two women, heedless of whether they could understand or not.

"To provide a brightly decorated bier and a warm grave is not the only thing the living can do for the dead. We must discover why he died. It's important. Someone's death brought the law and the police into being. Another's death provoked the creation of hospitals and of new medical studies. That's not all. By one person's death many other people can discover a new way of thinking, and writing, and living. Young Ch'ol-Hun's death is not simply the end either."

On returning to my room at the Savannah Hotel, I began to scrutinize his diary. He had started keeping it some two years before his death. The dates were inserted at random, sometimes nearly a whole month was passed over. Most of the contents were merely factual memos or things briefly noted down.

A happy man's diary is an empty one.

Someone with an unwritten diary enjoys a satisfying life; such people replenish their daily words by action.

The thickness of the leaves and the thickness of the action are ever in inverse proportion. No animal keeps a diary. I suppose that the same is true of God.

In every respect I hope that some day I will be able to go beyond the pages of this diary and really live a life worth living.

That was the inscription set at the top of the first page, like a series of epigrams. The following page was marked with the day of his father's death. The exact date was not noted, which suggested that it had happened long before he started to keep his diary.

I intended at first merely to skim through, just getting the gist, but once I reached the passage about his late father I found I could not bear to skip a single letter. It reminded me sharply of what I had heard from his sister.

People frequently write about returning to their family home dressed in silks and laden with honors. But our country home is no place for someone wearing silk robes to return to. People robed in silks don't need a home, anyway. In our home village, there is far more talk about people intent on hiding their grief-filled, filthy, tattered clothes than there is about people coming to show off silk robes.

People return to their former homes in sorrow. Our bodies are not the only things that turn homeward. Anyone who recalls their home while living in the city is surely weary of city life.

But being weary of city life is the same as being weary of life itself....

I went home to bury Father. Even when I got the telegram saying that he had suddenly died, I did not weep. Even when I was dressed in mourning clothes and standing before his coffin, no tears flowed. Was that because I felt too tense under the obligation to weep and keen?

For a son not to weep at his father's death is considered a sin against piety. Seeing the rest of the mourners, I made repeated attempts to weep. I wonder why I was unable to weep streams of tears like Mother?

I tried thinking of moving things so that tears might flow by association. I imagined the village school yard, empty except for the platform in front after school is over, our home's storage terrace in the rain, sparrows caught in a net, our village's desolate river bank, the bank where I used to read, draw pictures and sing, poplar trees with their branches bare.

It seemed that it was only in childhood that tears of emotion flow at the mere sight of branches high enough to touch the sky trembling in the breeze, and at the very thought of silent high noon with the splendor of green foliage.

I still could not cry. Those things no longer made my heart sad. I tried thinking of the fate of our ancestral home as it gradually fell into ruins, of its tiled roof overgrown with weeds and its collapsing wall, its ravaged garden, and the rusting handles on the gate. Father who had bought me a tricycle. Father who used to give me coins from his pocket. Father who used to play *paduk*, twist cords, clear his throat.... I tried imagining his various different faces. But I could feel no sorrow.

Just then I suddenly, quite abruptly, caught sight of a black chest looking rather like a coffin set beside the folding screen that concealed Father's body from view.

At that instant tears came welling up. It had been a long, long time since I had wept as I wept then. In a house of mourning, each and everyone is endowed with the freedom and the privilege to cry to their heart's content. It is because it is a place where tears are authorized that people unexpectedly find a kind of cheerful sense of relief rising up in them during a funeral.

"No, no! Those scoundrels. Don't they know whose land it is?"

From inside that chest I heard an echo of Father's voice as he strode through the village, shouting in protest.

The chest had belonged to him; it was a kind of Pandora's Box. Right up until his death he would not let it leave his side for a moment but kept a firm hold of it. I had even heard that his dying wish was that it should be buried with him.

Inside the chest were land titles and survey maps. Ah! Land, property, fields, and the red earth of the hills—only now the prescription had expired and Father had closed his eyes clinging on to a box full of useless land titles that were now nothing more than scrap paper.

Land has been our destiny. Land got my brother thrown out, land drove my father mad. From the very moment of Liberation, we had been the victims of land.

Land has been our destiny. We were a landowner's sons, who had no idea of how to survive without land. We, and I myself, belonged to the land. Now the land was taking its revenge on us. I spent my school days in terror and loneliness and gloom because I was "a son of the land." When I was dragged off by the children of the liberated tenants and whipped, I thought with sorrow of how much land Father owned.

"Now you aren't a *yangban* and this is not your land."

In order to test their new-found freedom, the tenants' children used to beat me up. The son of the ruined landowner came home every day with a bloody nose. The land divided me from my friends; it divided Father from my brother; and it divided the village folk from our family. By the time the War came in 1950, we had already lost all our lands but still Father was put to hard labor.

I don't have the heart to write about my brother. Even after the land was all gone, we were unable to get free of it. People vanished together with the land. One by one, the familiar faces vanished from our front gate.

Father only succumbed after struggling with all his might to prevent the loss of the land. As the doors to the visitors' quarters were shut, and dust began to gather in the rooms where kisaeng girls used to come and play, while the calligraphy on the boards fixed to the pillars melted away, and the trees in the garden, no longer pruned, ran wild, the deeds in that chest that Father clung onto turned into so much useless scrap paper.

Ah, that Pandora's Box that Hope never emerged from! How many sleepless nights Father had spent coughing as he guarded a chest where nothing remained but dust. In the end my brother too staked his youth on smashing that chest although what it contained was bound eventually to turn into waste paper without his lifting a finger. Whether it be the one intent on guarding, or the one intent on smashing, or the one just looking on, we were all of us forced to shoulder the same useless chest to the bitter end. We had nothing left except a chest full of expired titles and land registers. And now it was to be buried together with Father's body.

Mother asked me to read the inscriptions on the envelopes containing funeral contributions. Previously she had been weeping sadly, but now she was counting the money.

"From the family of Sok-Tol, one hundred *won*."

"That scum, and we used to let them farm the best rice fields too. How ungrateful can you get?"

"Here's two hundred *won* from the family of Ok-Sun."

"To think that we helped set her up with a place to live in when she got married and now look how rich they are. How dare they!"

"One thousand *won* from Chang-Pyo's folk!"

"A thousand? Chang-Pyo's father knew what was what. He was the only one able to recognize a kindness when he saw one. Naturally they still feel indebted to us, even the third generation."

I could not bear to read out any more of the names on the envelopes.

Mother! All those things are over now. Stop thinking about land. It's all over now Father's dead.

Mother was just like him, unable to escape from inside that chest full of dusty title deeds. She had no true sorrow capable of lifting her beyond those bitter sums of money. At the sight of Mother's face as she sat there counting money in her widow's garb, I once again tasted the salt of tears on my tongue.

Mother will never be able to get free. She will never be able to detach herself from the little patch of bald fields she inherited, and the memory of all that land. She's one of those people who can never leave home.

That was the end of the first section. I was incapable of going on to read anything more; the writing was so minute. I walked to the window in order to rest my weary eyes. It was already evening. Seen from this fifth floor room, Seoul lay grim and barren as if strewn with cinders. If you had thrown a stone down, the only result would have been a blurred cloud of dust.

The remains of some child's kite, the paper all torn away and the bamboo frame left like a skeleton, trembled in every puff of wind. The only thing I could distinguish clearly from this hotel window was the bathhouse on the edge of the hotel's front yard. The tall chimney rose like an extinct volcano, with not a trace of smoke issuing from it. The scars of machine-gun bullets from the war remained unrepaired. It would soon be demolished to make way for a car park. The window panes had all been smashed, so that the word "bath" originally written on them was nowhere fully legible. It looked as though it were being used as a temporary store. Piles of junk could be glimpsed through the windows.

The bathroom itself, where once naked bodies had loomed through billows of white vapor, was probably a mess of spider's webs and dust, broken bicycle wheels, desks, empty cans and beer bottles, and other trash. Out of the ruins one young fellow emerged. He was carrying a black wooden chest closed by a rusty padlock, issuing from the gloomy city's sticky alleys with their perpetual smell of rotting fish.

Perhaps he would never be able to free himself from the chest of bygone history. An inherited box that could never be removed from his shoulders: I was beholding Ch'ol-Hun's ghost, advancing laden like a snail with its house on its back.

Soon after I had turned on the lights in the room, Inspector Park came to see me. We shook hands easily, with no sign of hostility.

"Are you still thinking about this Kim Ch'ol-Hun business?"

As he spoke, Inspector Park tossed a college notebook on to the table. It must be the last section of Ch'ol-Hun's notebook that he had promised to show me.

"Aha, I see you've already read another part of his diary."

Inspector Park riffled through Ch'ol-Hun's diary where it lay on the table. I had the impression that he was smiling a victor's smile.

"Now I must tell you about my investigations."

I spoke without any intonation, imitating Inspector Park's way of talking.

"Have you discovered any reason why he might have committed suicide? At least there's one thing you ought to be careful about. In terms of seniority I'm above you, after all. You can't explicate the reasons for a suicide solely in terms of the event itself. Character as well as chance factors can call up the spirit of death. One person may kill himself for the price of a tram fare while another can loose billions and still not die. A widow can have her son die without being unduly affected, yet stuff herself with sleeping pills when her pet dog gets lost. Of course, I'm sure you know all about this kind of psychology. I'm just telling you some of my experiences for reference."

I answered, feeling increasingly confident that I could communicate with him.

"You're warning me that even if some kind of problem had come up, there's no proof it necessarily led him to kill himself. But..."

A call-boy came in, bringing a bottle of scotch and some glasses.

"But don't worry. So far my investigations are focused not so much on the cause of his death as on the creative reasons that made him want to write a novel called *The General's Beard.*"

"On why that one man could not bring himself to grow a beard when everyone else was doing it? Surely that's very simple."

Inspector Park was drinking his Johnny Walker straight.

"His mother says it was because he had that scar. While his sister, and she's a widow too...the last surviving offspring. She says it was because the shock he got was too severe when the brother he loved was arrested for political reasons. But if you look at his diary, he seems to suggest that it was because of his father's chest, where he kept all his title deeds."

"Novelists always complicate things. When you listen to them, the world seems wrapped in a thick fog. They turn the simplest things into riddles. That's why I always steered clear of literature."

What he said upset me, certainly, but my fingers did not shake like they had the day before, as they clasped the glass.

I defended my approach.

"It's not really a vague way of seeing things. I was simply speaking on the spur of the moment. At any rate, my investigation will continue."

This time it was Inspector Park's turn to defend himself.

"It only underlines the fact that we see this incident in differing ways. It has nothing to do with the question as to which of us is capable of seeing reality more clearly. But I'll have to pursue the interrogation that you so much dislike. How is it that you are suddenly so interested in the reasons for the death of someone when you said that you couldn't even remember his name? And in 'hours that people have paid you for'? I mean to say, it's going to waste more time than asking a leading question."

I did not reply at once but instead, for no particular reason, clinked my glass against his in a kind of toast.

"I recall that you already said that our points of view were different.... Why are the police so intent on finding reasons for his death? If someone killed him, you're going to have to find them. In order to repay the dead man's enemies? Surely not just that. You'll say it's in order to protect the legal order of things. For the sake of the people who are attached to the law with their every breath. If you say he killed himself, that's an end to your investigation. Only for us, and I suppose you're going to criticize that 'we' as being like a foggy day, for us that's the point at which our obligation to investigate the matter begins. The moment you say that the criminal isn't some precise individual wearing dark glasses, or carrying a 45-caliber revolver, or with a hideous scar on his face, it becomes all the more fascinating. We must capture and bring to justice that invisible criminal. For the sake of the people who are attached to life with their every breath. Whether it was a chest with the character for 'happiness' stuck on it, the mark of an iron on a forehead, or the calls of someone being taken away to prison one rainy night.... I feel convinced I have to find out who the criminal was that killed Kim Ch'ol-Hun. He was clearly deprived of his right to life by force."

I was drunk, doubtless from the effect of the whisky on an empty stomach. I mocked myself inwardly: You're getting to be quite a moralist.

From somewhere outside a patrol-car siren rose, continued, then died away. Yet another crime must have occurred.

3

I resolved to pursue my investigations calmly. Therefore I did not immediately start to read the final volume of Ch'ol-Hun's diary. The following morning, before returning to the hotel room, I spent some time sitting in a coffee-shop where the only records they played were the popular hits like Paul Anka's "Crazy Love" and Elvis Presley's "Kiss me Quick." I at once opened the note book.

The diary entries written just before his death began in epistolary style but then continued in a monologue. The text began with the name of a girl, Hyei.

November 24, cloudy, first snowfall
Hyei!
I received a letter from Mother a few days ago. If you had been with me, I would have read it aloud, like I used to.

Whenever I read Mother's letters, you used to laugh but I like reading her letters. I like the way she writes, using the old system of spelling that is the only one she knows. I can't imagine Mother writing a letter with the same kind of grammar and modern spelling that we use. She still uses one of the archaic characters in her letters, as if she were living back in the times of Ch'un-Hyang, and it is one of my little pleasures that they show how wrong it is to think that the old character can be represented with modern writing.

Hyei!

I'm worried about this letter of hers. As far as the style of address or the old-fashioned spelling goes, nothing has changed in the slightest. What bothers me is what she says.

She writes that she can't live in the countryside any longer. Even Mother has realized that the days are over when people employed laborers and farmhands to work the fields. Still, for a long time I've been convinced that she could never leave the land and our old home.

Hyei!

Like I told you before: because of that, I could always say that if I got tired of life I would go back home and work in the fields with Mother. Of course, I'm sure you realized that my words were lies, mere escapism. But the simple fact that I could imagine such a thing constituted a last straw of hope for me.

Hyei!

And now she writes that she is arriving in Seoul tomorrow. It seems that Kim So-Im has come forward and offered to buy the house, together with the remaining land.

I know his daughter well enough. Kim So-Im was one of our tenants back in the old days, too. Now his daughter is living with a G.I. It's as much as to say that our house, the house of Kim Chong-Taek of Chang-Dong, the great Kim clan, is going to become the home of a G.I.'s in-laws

Yet you know, Hyei, that's not the thing that has really upset me. That old house is too big and cumbersome, whether you look at it in terms of my unbearable memories or our widowed mother's life. The outer wing where the men used to receive visitors has already been turned into the village church, and the servants' quarters are being used as one political party's local offices.

It's a house that needs a new owner to take it over.

Hyei!

What I'm afraid of is that my last bastion of self-defense has disappeared, the possibility of saying, "Well, I can always go back to our village and farm with mother, can't I?" I'm not sure that saying I'm living here with mother will be the same thing at all. In mathematical terms, it makes no difference whether you say mother's coming to me or I'm going to mother. But in the light of what our lives have been like, I reckon that saying mother is coming to me and saying that I am going to mother mean something fundamentally different.

After that, for the space of about half a page, the writing had all been crossed out until nothing was legible. The diary entry continued on the following page.

Hyei!

I've done another stupid thing. Mother is going to come up by train tomorrow to talk about getting rid of the house. So just now I called the enquiries desk at Seoul station.

There I was, holding the telephone and explaining how Mother was coming up from the countryside to sell our land, and that I reckoned it would be hard for her to find where I lived on her own, so that I'd better go to meet her off the train.

At that point the girl on enquiries interrupted me in an angry voice, asking what on earth I was talking about. Get straight to the point...it's nothing to do with me whether it's your mother who's coming up or your grandmother, whether she's selling some land or a whole mountain. She sounded furious.

Hyei! Don't laugh at me. I've always been like that. She was right. They're busy people. The fact that Mother is selling the house our people have lived in for three generations and moving to the city can signify nothing to anyone except me.

Hyei! That wasn't the last of my mistakes. Hastily changing the topic, I enquired what time the train from Pusan would arrive at Seoul tomorrow. I would have to be there to meet her.

At that I heard the girl heave a sigh and mutter to herself something about how country people always made her sick. There were dozens of trains arriving from Pusan every day; which particular train was I asking about, for heaven's sake? Was I asking her to sit there reading out the whole day's list? And she hung up.

Hyei! What she said was perfectly correct. Not having indicated the time of the train may have been Mother's mistake or mine, it was clear that it was entirely our mistake.

I'll have to go out early to Seoul station tomorrow. I'm going to have to spend the whole day pressed against the barrier at the exit from the platforms, with all those people swarming around me.

There'll be any number of mothers coming up to Seoul from the countryside. I'm going to have to explore hundreds, thousands of mothers' faces as they come pouring out in procession. I'll have to distinguish Mother's face in all that mass.

I'll spend the whole day there tomorrow, the whole day standing there. I'll have to wait there all day long, exploring, among the footsteps of people dashing off in a hurry, the eyes of total strangers.

Only he had not waited; he had died. He was dead when his mother arrived. Could death have been what he had been waiting for all that time? Surely that was what he was waiting for, gazing at those mothers' faces, among the footsteps of people dashing off in a hurry, the eyes of total strangers!

In any case, on reading that I began to wonder if it might not have been suicide after all. Perhaps this girl that he had been writing to had understood Ch'ol-Hun's feelings? Hyei?

Could she be the girl that Inspector Park said had been living with him for six months, whose alibi and background he said were clear? I felt a desire to meet her. For that, I would need Inspector Park's help. I decided to phone him. I had the impression that since I had now read the very beginning and the very end of the diary, I would do well to meet people and get some more tangible information before continuing to read the remaining diary entries.

4

I got an urgent call from my publisher, demanding to know how the manuscript was coming along. Seeing that it was meant to be about the Christmas season and it was going to be late, they supposed I had almost finished writing. But I had done absolutely nothing about it. Nothing was written. It looked likely that I would not be able to write anything today either. As soon as I had eaten the "continental breakfast" supplied by the hotel, I set off for the office block where, following Inspector Park's instructions, I hoped to find Miss Na Shin-Hyei.

The building in question stood in the main business area stretching along Chongno Street. It was a dark, old-fashioned cement construction that had not been redecorated for a long time. Even in broad daylight, all the lights were burning. In the lobby, an old porter, blind in one eye, was shaking his hands and quarrelling with a cleaning woman about something. There was an elevator, but it was an antique model of a 1930s kind, with a sign stuck to the gates that said: "Power failure, not in use." With all the lights on, despite the sign, it looked as if the elevator girl had got the sack, or the thing had broken down. Behind the elevator gates with their peeling paintwork, a cavernous dark space yawned like an abyss.

The girl worked in an estate agent's office on the fifth floor. I steeled myself to climb the exiguous stairways, where it looked as if I would have to be careful not to bang my head. At every landing as I climbed, my eyes encountered the dark cavern looming beyond the elevator gates with the sign "Power failure, not in use."

In the office, one solitary woman was sitting among empty desks. I had heard reports that there were many companies with just their administrative offices in the buildings in the region of Chongno. It looked as though this estate agent were one of them.

The woman was filing her nails and before I could ask anything informed me: "The chairman is out. He won't be back today." I had the impression that she was reading a speech from a prepared text.

Only her immense eyes, dark eyes in which black flames seemed to be flickering, held an ardor incapable of indifference about anything. Her makeup was not particularly elaborate. Perhaps that explained why her eyes were so conspicuous.

"I'm not interested in meeting the chairman; I want to meet Na Shin-Hyei. Is she around...could I perhaps see her?"

I asked in this indirect way although intuitively I felt sure that this woman must be Na Shin-Hyei herself.

"Are you from the police? Do I have to go with you now?"

She showed no trace of anxiety. Her voice sounded clear and young. She put her handbag and her desk in order. I said nothing in reply to her question as to whether I was from the police.

"Some coffee-shop nearby would be convenient; that is, if you can leave the office."

We were obliged to go down all those stairs. Naturally the sign "Power failure, not in use" was fixed to the gates of the elevator. The young woman went ahead of me. She wore her hair in a ponytail, like a student, tightly tied with a scarlet ribbon that made a vivid contrast with the black of the hair. It was a style favored by younger students, and not really suitable for someone of her age.

"You and Kim Ch'ol-Hun lived together, so...um..."

As soon as we were in the coffee-shop, I began to question her like a real detective.

"You don't have to be embarrassed. I lived with him for six months. That's what I told them at the station."

I was completely taken by surprise. She spoke frankly, in open, unaffected tones. She seemed to be inviting me to ask whatever I liked. Most women avoid meeting a man's eyes when they are speaking. Usually while they are talking they look at their wrist-watch, or stare into the distance over their partner's shoulder, or something of that kind. But as this woman spoke, she was scrutinizing each portion of my face with those almond eyes in which black flames seemed to be flickering.

Normally a person who knows no shame has no authenticity either. But Shin-Hyei seemed to possess such purity that not even a devil could have made her fall. I reflected that you sometimes come across a mysterious kind of woman who remains a virgin even after losing her virginity. I felt reassured as I interpreted her character. If she were like that, I would have to be completely open with her.

"I'm not an inspector from the police at all. But I'm someone who needs your testimony, yes, your testimony, much more than they do. I'm writing a novel."

Shin-Hyei seemed to smile slightly.

"Are you looking for materials? It seems that writing a novel with imagination only is hard as well."

"As well? What do you mean?" I quickly questioned her.

"Because there once was a man who thought he could love a woman with just his imagination."

"You're talking about Kim Ch'ol-Hun?"

"He only wanted to love me in his fantasies. He did all he could to escape from the real me, the me that bleeds if I'm scratched, and snores when I sleep. The only things he cared about in life were his own dreams. When I was in front of him, I had the impression that I was vanishing into thin air like petrol evaporating. I reckon it takes more than imagination to write a novel, so do you think a man and a woman can go on loving one another deeply using only their imaginations?"

"I want to hear all the details of your story in their proper order. Don't you find this music rather loud?"

The waitress came over.

"I'll have tea."

"That gramophone music..."

"Leave it as it is. It's better loud."

Shin-Hyei looked at her watch. Then she began by explaining that she wanted to get everything off her chest. With the way the police asked questions, it was like having to explain the marks left by a cart-wheel without mentioning the cart or the wheel. However, she really wanted at least once to be able to tell someone what their relationship had been like. She added that it would be better with a stranger like me.

"I had a wretched and strange...or rather, the fact that I had a very peculiar father and that before we met I lost my virginity in a rather melodramatic manner must have been what attracted him to me. I think I can draw that conclusion quite confidently."

She had lived an almost hopeless existence. At the time when she met Ch'ol-Hun, she was working as a dancer in a back-room dance-hall, depending entirely on the tips she got from the customers. It was one of those February days when you could feel the first signs of spring. Shin-Hyei had got off with a man claiming to be a company director and they were dancing together. Suddenly they heard the door being broken down and a group of about ten young men came bursting in. They were being raided by a plain-clothes police squad.

Shin-Hyei had not run away. She simply stood there laughing at the sight of the chasing, running, vases smashing, people being arrested, while all the while, from the gramophone that no one had bothered to stop, issued the strains of a tango, "La Cumparsita." She had finally been arrested too. But she had the impression that she was like the music that had gone on playing, indifferent to all around it, that she dwelt in the same world apart as music inhabited. The fat businessman she had been dancing with was trying to hide his terrified face with a towel. Cameramen from the press, given the tip-off in advance, were busily firing off their flash bulbs.

Once outside, Shin-Hyei began to worry about her father. He was at home, half-paralyzed, waiting for his daughter to come back. He spent his life lying there like some insect, unable so much as to turn over on his own. If she didn't come home within a few days, only a few days, he would be starving, staring up at the ceiling and reciting the Lord's Prayer.

That was how it had been during the war, when Shin-Hyei had come back up to Seoul after it was liberated. Her father was lying prostrate on the wooden floor of his rectory. Pastor Na, the victim of a stroke, lay there like a corpse, simply staring up at the ceiling. He had been tortured by political security agents from the North.

As soon as she thought of her father, she began to tremble with apprehension. She opened her bag, took out her lipstick, and hastily scribbled something on a slip of paper. A sketch of where her house was, with the address. She quickly jotted down a few words: "Please, it's my father. I'll make it up to you when I get out." She thought how the little note was like a message thrown to the winds. She tossed the note to a photographer who was taking shots of her face.

"Please, I beg you."

She was already being dragged toward the police van as she spoke.

Returning home after three days in the cells, she found all the lights on, while her father and that journalist were engaged in friendly conversation.

"He was on very close terms with Father. They had obviously talked together a lot. He had even taken care of his bodily functions, something that normally only a son can do."

I sucked the last cold dregs of my coffee as I listened to Shin-Hyei's tale.

"I suppose that your father was preaching to Ch'ol-Hun?"

"Not at all. Father never used to try to preach to anyone once he was outside the church. That was not his way."

Shin-Hyei pulled down the neck of her sweater so that I could see her necklace. It was a copper cross.

"Father gave me this cross as he was dying, as a kind of last bequest. He was a clergyman, yet he never liked the idea of me attending Sunday school. Once I was a bit older he told me to stop going to church. He said that usually the more you know God, the further you go from him; that if people start to feel what God is like, they become unhappier and then, unable to overcome the resulting stress and anguish, they end up hating

God. He told me that if you wanted to keep God from being cursed, the best way was to live without knowing him. He even said that blaspheming God was a much worse thing than not knowing him."

The little copper cross propped on her hands shone reflected in Shin-Hyei's eyes with their flickering black flames.

"Your father must have regretted becoming a pastor."

"Not at all. To his last breath he used to say quite peacefully that he breathed every breath quietly in company with God. Only he had to endure a tremendous struggle. 'Ah, Shin-Hyei!' he told me, 'There may not be one man in ten thousand capable of gaining the victory in my kind of battle and winning through to God. It's no easy thing for an innocent man to keep believing in God when he has lost a wife and children. Most Christians put on masks of falsehood and lie in order to escape such sufferings, and cause God to be cursed.' He had lost his wife and two sons. Besides, he was quite exceptionally unlucky as well. That was the kind of father Ch'ol-Hun liked. Abandoned, paralyzed, completely ignored by everyone, lying shut up in a tiny room like a corpse, that was the father he liked."

She told how at first she had felt revolted by Ch'ol-Hun's kindness.

"Why did you pay any attention to the unlikely request of someone like me, a dancer you'd never seen before, a loose woman being taken away by the police? Was it because the dancer said she'd make it up to you? Or do you make a vile hobby of dishing out pity to people?"

She admitted that instead of thanking him she began to pick a quarrel.

"No, it's nothing like that. I simply remembered what one human being shouted desperately as she was being carted off, dragged away like a dog by the police. I'd have done it for anyone, even if you'd been a murderer. I could hear those hastily scribbled words written in blood-red lipstick crying out like your voice in the rainy night. Now I have to thank you. I have never before been able to talk as open-heartedly as I have with Pastor Na. He needed my help. It was only a short period, just three days, but during that time, I always knew if he wanted a drink, or had to do his needs, or felt bored and wanted to talk, even without asking. Shin-Hyei! We talked so much! We talked and talked, like shipwrecked fishermen meeting on a desert island. Without the electric light, but using that oil lamp, hearing it hiss and give off a stink of paraffin. We talked far into the night. You know, Shin-Hyei, I had a terrible time finding this house with just the address. Your house lay high up on some hill, like Kafka's 'Castle' and I couldn't find the path leading up to it. But now, after three days going up and down that path, I've found out where it leads."

Shin-Hyei forced herself to put on a smile.

"He used to exaggerate about everything."

She tried to make it sound unimportant, but I saw the black flames come flickering brightly into her eyes.

I told her to keep on talking, employing Inspector Park's technique of interrogation.

"Did you understand what he was feeling?"

"I was thinking what a shame it was he had that scar on his forehead. Because I had the same kind of scar; I could sense that he wasn't one of those brash types who tell a girl straight out that they want to make love. He told me that he saw his scar as a 'token of solitude,' guaranteeing that he could never hurt anyone. Ours was a relationship that was doomed from the start not to become a real one."

"Did he often come visiting after that?"

"Almost every day. He came virtually every day, explaining that he had been intending to change his job anyway. He liked us, but it was impossible to tell if it was father or me that he liked more. Father used to be waiting for him, too. Of the three of us, I was the only one relatively indifferent toward him."

So Ch'ol-Hun had come almost every day to Shin-Hyei's house. To Shin-Hyei he said that he would be getting another job soon, and that she should take it easy in the meantime. He kept pestering the indifferent Shin-Hyei to keep her promise and "make it up" to him. When she asked him what he wanted in return, he asked her to reveal to him some secret that she had never told anyone, to show him something invisible like the scar on his forehead. He was suggesting they should play at being each other's father confessor.

Shin-Hyei asked him what kind of game he thought he was playing, that she considered telling your secrets to other people to be as disgusting as showing them your underwear. He insisted that it didn't have to be that kind of thing, but that they would grow closer by telling each other things that they had never before told a living soul. Ch'ol-Hun proposed that he should begin by telling her about the scar on his forehead.

Shin-Hyei paused and smiled shyly.

"It really was a droll kind of game. We kept playing similar games all the time we were together. The one listening would sit somewhere a bit higher up, on a chair or a table or a window-sill, while the person telling the secret would sit below and talk with closed eyes. He would pester and badger me like a baby with his 'Right! let's play confessions.'"

That first day, Shin-Hyei had sat astride a rock up on the hill while Ch'ol-Hun leaned against a young pine tree and spoke. On later inspection, it turned out that the entry in his diary for February 18 reproduced that first make-believe confession to Shin-Hyei in the form of a monologue.

Shin-Hyei! I had no friends. Ours was a *yangban* family and father was a landowner. The rest of the village kids were all the children of vulgar farm laborers, servants and serfs. The fact that I was the landowner's son, and the grandson of a high minister, was stamped on me even earlier than the brand from the hot iron on my brow, from the day of my birth.

I was born like that. When the other kids were out catching snakes, I would stand watching a good way off, all alone. I longed to join in with them, but I was not as good at those things as they were. The kids went wading through fields of mud, getting themselves bitten by leeches as they caught loaches. I merely watched them from my vantage-point, perched on a farmhand's back.

If mother ever asked, "Why can't you join in and play with the other children?" I used to tell her it was because they said bad things about the scar on my forehead. There was that as well, of course. I had simply been born different from the children who went rolling in the muddy fields to their hearts' content.

Shin-Hyei, even when I tried to act like them, I couldn't. I did join with them and take part in stealing baby sparrows from their nests, but there was one boy, called Il-Pyo, who was an absolute demon at wheedling the baby sparrows out from their nests inside the straw thatch of the houses. He would climb a ladder and pull out the chicks one by one. Then he would hand them down to the other children who were gazing up from below. One day I found myself holding one too.

Ah, Shin-Hyei! Why couldn't I? Why was I unable to keep hold of that baby sparrow, when everyone else was quite calmly holding theirs? No sooner had I held that clammy sparrow chick with its feathers not yet sprouting than I threw it to the ground, nearly fainting. The kids laughed at me and called me a coward, but it gave me the creeps to such an extent that I could not endure to touch it.

It wasn't only while I was small, Shin-Hyei!

THE GENERAL'S BEARD

The day my older brother was arrested—he taught me a lot, you know, drawing, singing, skating, taking photos, and that means my present job, too—from the time he was arrested I found it even more impossible to associate with other people. And something taught me there was a clear meaning in my being alone, in being alone with myself.

Shin-Hyei! It was—Shin-Hyei, just listen—it was one day when we were on a middle school outing. We went to visit Magok Temple. The other pupils in my class were forming little groups with their closest friends and having their pictures taken with the temple's main hall in the background. You paid your money and the school photographer took the pictures. Only you know, there was no group where I belonged. No one wanted to fit me in and I couldn't find any kids worth fitting in with. I was alone, alone... Standing blankly beside the photographer, I watched the other kids getting their pictures taken, baring their white teeth and pushing back their shoulders. There was not one that called me over to have my photo taken with them.

Shin-Hyei, that was the first time that a sense of shame overcame me. The sense that I could not fit into any group and had to walk alone, all by myself. I took off and hid in the valley behind the temple, where I lay with my feet in the stream. I stared up at the sky, listening to the sound of the other kids chattering in the distance. The sky was really high above. I thought that I was floating along like a cloud. And that tale by Anderson, my favorite one, about the swan that hatched among the ducks, I thought of that too. Then I fell asleep.... Shin-Hyei! I only woke up when I heard all the children calling out my name in a kind of chorus: "Ch'ol-Hun, where are you? Ch'ol-Hun, where are you?"

Fifty or sixty people were calling my name. It was already evening. Checking that all were present at the moment of setting off down the hill, they realized I had vanished and the other kids were scouring the hills in search of me. Hearing the entire class calling my name, I felt happy. But my happiness was very short-lived. I was duly thrashed by the sports teacher in front of the assembled pupils. They looked on with contemptuous expressions.

Shin-Hyei! What happened that day made me more miserable than ever. I may not have been with them, but I belonged among them. I mean, I was one of their number. After all, even if I wanted to get free, even if I tried to get as far away as possible from them, there was no escaping the fact that I was one of their total number.

Shin-Hyei! Can you imagine what it felt like? Because of me, my classmates were obliged to go home thirty minutes late and because of that I found myself further from them than ever. Just thinking of it makes me go nearly crazy. Besides, it all happened only two months after my brother was taken away, and I was in a sickly state. That incident has pursued me ever since, like the scar on my brow. People showed no interest in me. I was a complete outsider, but they could never be content simply to leave me alone.

Shin-Hyei! Be patient just a little bit longer. It must be boring but my confession is nearly over. It's nothing important, only you're the first person I've ever told it to. Suppose we abolish completely every last secret between us, do you suppose we can become utterly one? Ah! A single body. Can two people ever become completely one, do you think? I want to believe in such a miracle. Then I went to do my military service. There I could feel it clearly; I was separate from them, and at the same time I was part of them. It became obvious whenever the whole platoon got punished for my particular mistake, or I for someone else's mistake. They gave me the nickname "Councilor." Councilor...that's what they call people in the army who are outsiders, odd-men-out. I tried hard to make friends, to understand them, did all I could to get in among them, but it was no good. Out on that wide parade ground, even when we were in line together, keeping step together, arm-in-arm as we did our training, I was alone just like when I stood at the water's edge while the kids caught loaches.

Still, Shin-Hyei! I did make just one friend. He was born into the royal clan, his name was Yi Jin. He spoke to me first. He remarked that it's people's weak points that bring them together. That friendships fostered by weaknesses like drinking or gambling or vice are stronger than any inspired by morality or shared birthplace. He told me he reckoned that society was all rotten; this generation had reached a point where they all lived like gangsters, so that especially in the army, the only way you could get close to them was by mastering the art of swearing. He was certainly a master at swearing richly in a most unroyal manner. He was right. If you wanted to become part of them, you had to start by changing your way of speaking.

You know, Shin-Hyei, I really tried. Don't laugh. I made a conscious effort to use the expressions that they were always using. But the problem was that it wasn't natural for me as it was with them. When I tried to swear, for some reason everybody laughed. I was incapable of reeling off whole strings of oaths like them. Now Shin-Hyei, I'm going to end this last part of my confession with a really terrible, fateful incident.

It involves that friend who told me I ought to learn to swear. Yi Jin, I mean. He got himself killed because of me.

There had been a lull with no fighting. We were resting at the side of some paddy-fields. Suddenly a communist plane appeared, flying low and firing its machine guns. I took cover in the sluice pierced in the side of the rice-field, which was just large enough for one person. Only you see, Yi Jin couldn't find anywhere to run to. He was hovering in confusion up on the bank. He was in danger.

I was fond of Yi Jin. I felt he was like me. I dashed out, dragged him down, and forced him into the sluice where I had been hiding. Then I crouched down low on the bank nearby, although it was dangerous.

When the strafing was over, I went back to the sluice. Yi Jin! It's OK now, you can come out! I shouted as I went, so glad I was to be alive.

Ah, Shin-Hyei! You know how I found Yi Jin? He was bleeding. Inside that sluice where I had been kneeling, in that sluice that I had believed would be safer than anywhere else, he was dying. He was calling my name as he died. With eyes rolled up so that the whites showed, he kept asking for me. It's your fault I'm dying! He seemed to be saying. Shin-Hyei...that was the result of my self-sacrificing friendship. Because of me, he got the bullet aimed at me.

Shin-Hyei, that is my confession. Now it's your turn. I'll sit up on the rock.

Shin-Hyei raised her head. The flames had died out in her eyes and darkness was spreading over them. She was holding a sheet of silver paper from a pack of cigarettes that she kept crumpling up then smoothing out; she spoke as if she were in a dream.

"Aren't you tired? I've just been chattering on idly. I don't seem to have told you any of the things you want to know. That's how it always is when people speak."

I sensed that Shin-Hyei did not want to talk any more, but I was curious about how Ch'ol-Hun had been when they broke up.

"I want to know why he killed himself. I want to get to the bottom of the motives and reasons he had for doing it. All I've heard so far does nothing more than explain why he was alone. There must have been something more that had an effect on him. No bell rings by itself."

"Why, you belong to the same group as Inspector Park. Will you be satisfied if I tell you it was because I left him?"

There was a sudden commotion at the coffee-shop counter. There seemed to be some bother between the waitress and a drunk.

"I say I paid for the phone call. Besides, it was only two *won*."

"I said I didn't get it because I didn't, that's all."

The two of them continued to repeat the same words in increasingly loud tones.

"Let's get out of here. Next time.... I'd rather we talked of important things next time. It's been too sudden; I've got a headache."

Shin-Hyei stood up. The cross at her breast shone brightly.

5

For the next few days, my head was full of thoughts of Kim Ch'ol-Hun.

Why did he suddenly die? If it wasn't suicide, was it homicide as Inspector Park had said? Should I meet Shin-Hyei again? I was curious as to why they had broken up, and what had been Kim Ch'ol-Hun's attitude at the time of their breakup. Yet I had the impression that if I went carefully through the notes in his diary, I would be able to get the overall picture. I was about to plunge into his notebooks again when I received a phone call from Inspector Park. They had found Ch'ol-Hun's camera in a tiny second-hand store in the Eastgate Market. A woman had sold it to them for next to nothing a few days earlier. He joked that he was sorry, but it looked as though he were going to get to the bottom of the riddle of why he had died before I did.

That was how close we had been brought by Kim Ch'ol-Hun's death. I made a joke in return, to the effect that we would no doubt end up by getting a full picture of the criminal solitude that had killed him, but that he would never be able to arrest or charge it....

I turned to the February entries in his diary. The tale of his "confession game" was written under the date February 18. From the contents it became clear that the confession game had not been his own invention, and that he had based it on a hint from a scene in Marcel Carné's film "Dangerous Turning." What was more interesting was the way that Shin-Hyei, too, had taken part in the game she said was so entertaining.

Thanks to what he wrote about their game, I was able to confirm the correctness of my previous surmise that what had attracted him to Shin-Hyei was the melodramatic manner in which she had lost her virginity. After describing what he had confessed, the notes went on to summarize the contents of her confession to him. Here and there he had inserted comments of his own in brackets. There was of course no way I could be sure if his record was exact.

February 23

Shin-Hyei sat where I had been, leaning against the pine tree, and gazed up at me.

"I represent humanity. I'm the priest representing humanity, here to receive your confession. But you can be sure that I'll keep your secret as safe as my own life."

I had the impression that I was about to grow dizzy at the sight of Shin-Hyei's mysterious eyes gazing up at me. She hesitated for a moment, then began to speak.

"There is just one fact that Father knows nothing about. And it's something so melodramatic that it's positively indecent.

But I'll tell you. In fact, I wish you would explain it. Because really it was a completely meaningless incident."

"Come on, Shin-Hyei, tell me about it."

I felt prickly with anticipation; I had the impression I was developing a chill. She closed her eyes.

We kept walking further and further from Seoul. It was early in January of 1951, during the retreat from Seoul, when my melodrama began. It was freezing. Father had told me to get away from the city. There will be persecutions, he said, and since that would include you, you must leave. I set out for Pusan with another student, a boy from next door who had just entered university. In Pusan there was a friend's house, a girl I had gone to school with, whose father was a pastor of the same denomination as my father.

I'll tell it very simply, without any frills. I was in love with that student and he was infatuated with me. It didn't feel like an evacuation; it was more like a merry picnic. Yet there was a war going on, and it was bitterly cold. We were cold and lonely, yet I refused to let him come near me. It was often very inconvenient, because it meant we couldn't share the same room, but still...

And although I was extremely fond of him, I kept on exhorting him, more like an adult, explaining that I had to stay chaste. He used to reply that it was wartime and that bullets don't avoid the young. Father, you must treat all this as a joke. (Is she really laughing? Probably it's to avoid too much tension. I'm afraid that I spoke too plaintively during my confession.)

Father! It's as if war were designed to make people jealous of young people's pure beautiful love. It's as if war only picked on youth. It was a kind of silent threat. What he was asking for was different from what some playboy might want. He told me plainly: before he died, before the god of war called him, he wanted to possess me. But Father, how old do you think I was? I was too young. At my age, just looking and smiling and talking was enough.

Don't laugh now, Father. You see, his prophecy came true. And it all happened much too soon. He was grabbed as we were walking along, pulled up onto a military truck, and driven away. There I was, all alone. He wore glasses with thick lenses but war has no time to take account of things like the power of a person's glasses. I continued on in the column of unfamiliar refugees until I reached the town of Chochiwon, by which time my feet were so swollen with chilblains that I could not walk another step.

Father! What do you think I did then? (Poor Shin-Hyei...) I fell in with a group of women refugees from the factories of Yongdung-po, just south of Seoul. They said there was a possibility of getting to Pusan on board a military freight train. They told me to follow them and not ask any questions. They seemed to have struck up a relationship with the soldiers guarding the station. It was night. We crept into the station precincts and hid in a freight car with no locomotive attached. Would it really leave? Where was it headed? How long would we have to wait inside it?

Father! Ch'ol-Hun! (She suddenly began to tremble. I guessed that something terrible had happened to her there. Poor Shin-Hyei! War is no picnic. So much can be forgiven. I longed to embrace her. But as soon as I moved, she made a gesture as if pushing me away, warning me to stay where I was.)

My chilblains were itching so much I couldn't sleep. Unlit trains were rattling past, spouting smoke. Then we were discovered by some American soldiers. I was grabbed by a black soldier, who dragged me away to the fuel-yard where coal lay in mounds. It was already daybreak. In one corner of the coal-yard there was a kind of sentry-box with walls neatly made of straw sacking. I screamed and struggled but my youth was at an end.

In the pale dawn light, I gazed about me in search of help. There was no one in sight. All I could see, tied to one side of a shed not far from where I lay, was a mule loaded with what looked like military supplies, staring vacantly in my direction. A very scrawny mule. I made a sign with my hand in the direction of the mule, as if it were a human being. The mule was looking into my eyes. The eyes of that animal, completely ignorant of everything, were twinkling like the dawn stars against the pale gray of the sky.

I didn't cry. At the same time as I dusted off my skirt, stained black with the coal dust covering the yard, I brushed away forever my youth, my love, my dreams. The black soldier was flashing white teeth and smiling. I was fainting, nearly unconscious.

When I opened my eyes, the train was moving. Beyond the barred windows I could see snow-covered barley fields. The women workers had come back too. They were rejoicing at their good luck, feeling that now everything would be all right. It turned out that they had known all along what would happen; it was an implicit condition that had only been kept concealed from me.

Some of them comforted me with the thought that it was better than freezing to death. I had given up my virginity in exchange for a train ticket, that's right, a ticket. I sat there in that freight train, inwardly making apologies to the student—to that student who maybe was dead by now.

That's all. That's all the secrets I've got.

I had become an adult, hardened; I heard a door closing. There was no one who would ever be able to open it again. The key had been thrown out of the train into the mounds of coal, back there in the coal-yard. Human eyes vanished from my sight; I could see nothing but the eyes of the mule, staring blankly at me as I pleaded and did my utmost to call for help. And the mule's breath steaming about its mouth...

Thank you, Ch'ol-Hun; the day when I wrote that letter with my lipstick and ventured to call for help, I seem to have encountered human eyes for the first time in many years. (Shin-Hyei! I embraced you wildly. You were trembling. There's nothing to be afraid of. There's two of us. We can't just look on like that mule. Not if we open human eyes. We've opened human eyes and we're watching over each other, aren't we? I hugged you until there was no space left between us anywhere. I was thirty and it was the first time I had ever been able to embrace a woman.)

I had a feeling that I could understand why Ch'ol-Hun had come to like Shin-Hyei. In her eyes with their flickering black flames lay the entrance to a secret passage piercing the thick wall that separated him from other people, and that was what it was. It must have seemed like an emergency exit—the passage he had been looking for.

The more I perused Ch'ol-Hun's diary, the more I had the impression that unclear points were sorting themselves out. The virginity that Shin-Hyei had lost so melodramatically must have seemed to him like a wound. He had pried that wound open, trying to delve down into her heart. Ch'ol-Hun must always have longed for someone else's wound to match with his own.

Under another date, he wrote something to just that effect.

Yi Jin knew something important. He taught me that if people want to blend closely, they must commit a crime together: drinking, or gambling, or vice...it's true, things like that have the power to unite people closely. Yet there was something he didn't know.

There was something important that he didn't know: that the unity based on evil is an ideal, and nothing more. Those bonds are like shadows that melt and vanish in the rays of the rising sun.

For someone to become truly one with another person, they must touch one another's aching wounds. I'll never be able to become a Christian like Pastor Na. But now I understand. If Jesus was able to become one with his disciples and all mankind, it's because of the wounds left in his hands by the nails. Jesus told Thomas, when he wouldn't believe in the Resurrection, to stretch out his hand and touch the print of the nails and the wound left by the spear in his side.

Just what is a wound, then? What is the wound gaping in the soul's inmost darkness? If you know that, you can become close friends even with total strangers. We are not special like Jesus. But we live with just the same kind of scars as he has. We can't show a miracle of resurrection like Jesus, but we have exactly the same proof of resurrection as Jesus—those fresh scars. Pastor Na taught me the meaning of my wound, and I enabled Shin-Hyei to touch that wound. I am no longer lonely.

Ch'ol-Hun had been alienated from other people and at the same time had himself turned his back on others. He was afraid of "people" and was reluctant to associate with them. Especially after seeing the way his attempt to help Yi Jin had caused his death, he seemed to have become more convinced than ever about just how little he should mix with people.

Naturally, it was not clear what difference it made that he had met Pastor Na before meeting his daughter. What psychological effect did Pastor Na have on him? It took some trouble, but I studied carefully the diary entries from the thirteenth of February until the eighteenth. That was the time when, at Shin-Hyei's request, he had met Pastor Na. But his notes were rather different from what I had expected. There was nothing noted about any direct psychological change in himself. All I found was a quite objective account of what Pastor Na told him, and of their conversations, written like the script for a play.

My head was heavy, but I felt that I had to read carefully what Pastor Na had told him. His handwriting was very small and in many places the ink had run. The first part dealt with his impressions of Pastor Na, the later part related what he had said.

How does Pastor Na manage to look so peaceful even when he's alone, as if he had company? Everything around him was bleak, yet he seemed to be out playing with baby angels in fragrant fields. It must really be true that physical sufferings can have no direct effect on the mind.

He cannot deny that he is alone. For years he's been just lying there like a corpse. Probably visitors, his faithful parishioners, used to come at first and sing hymns. But would anyone go on and on caring for that body slowly sinking into death? He must have realized that people were leaving him one by one and he must have felt solitude increasingly crowding into his breast, as if eager to be present at his death.

But he makes his solitude serve him. He reckons that his solitude has a halo around it. Wouldn't I be happy too, if I could be strong like that when I'm on my own? Even though he's all alone, he looks like someone with a lot of friends.

(...)

Pastor Na spoke with a voice light as the early morning sunlight, and pure as that of a newborn babe. Anyone hearing him who claimed he was a fraud or a hypocrite could only be an agent of the devil.

When their physical tortures failed to work, they found a different method to torment me. It was really very intelligent of them. They turned to psychological torture. Using children. One five, the other nine, the sons of one of our church's deacons. They tied me to a chair in such a way that I could not turn my head away. Then, what do you think? They started to torture those children before my very eyes.

You can't imagine what it was like, their screams, and the blood seeping from their infant bodies. Then they spoke to me: We're going to torture these kids until you open your mouth and talk. You're a pastor, and you're supposed to love people, save innocent souls, and help people. It's your fault these children are being hit. Then they told the children: Plead to the pastor, then maybe we'll stop hitting you. Don't plead to us. Ask your pastor for pity; he's so fond of you.

Ah! Do you think I could endure it? If I spoke, I would be handing over to capture and death two of our church's young members who had trusted me and told me their secret. I had sworn to God not to tell a living soul where they were hiding. Yet if I remained silent, those completely innocent children were going to go on suffering torture before my very eyes.

I thought over every part of the scriptures. But it was nowhere written how we ought to act in that kind of situation. I came near to blaspheming against God then. I was repeating over and over, like Jesus on the cross: *"Eli, eli, lama sabachtani?* Why have you forsaken me?" The children could not stand the beating and were on their knees before me, pleading. "Pastor, save us. We won't play games in church again." Yet I ground my teeth and refused to speak. They had been able to tell me their hiding place because they trusted me.

Don't you see? It was a trust so sacred that nobody, nobody I say, could touch it.

Then finally I spoke. Those children were there before me, desperately begging one last time, when I realized that the others were just as heartless as the men who were beating up the children. And then, would you believe it, there were those two brothers dabbing away at one another's wounds, no doubt thinking there was no one they could rely on except one another. The nine-year-old was wiping the blood from his little brother's cheeks and stroking his hair, while the five-year-old wiped away his brother's tears and hugged him. Oh, God! (Tears were pouring from Pastor Na's hitherto peaceful eyes. He paused for a moment, perhaps wanting to pray.)

My friend! I broke my promise. I spoke. I am not sure I would have found peace if that had been the end of the matter. But when they arrived at the address I had given them, the young men weren't there. They had moved somewhere else as soon as they heard I had been arrested. They had not trusted my promise to them. They were safe because they trusted nobody. I knew they were only being sensible, that they had no choice, and after all, I had betrayed their trust. Yet somehow I felt sad to think that they had not trusted me, and had gone somewhere else.

The men from the North thought I had lied to them, and laid into me for all they were worth, demanding to know the real address. Inwardly I was letting go of all my bitterness. Young friend! Don't think I'm being hypocritical. At the pain I felt as they beat me, my heart grew calm and instead I rejoiced. If they had not beaten me, I would have beaten myself. As a result I was crippled, but inside I'm at peace, and my heart is completely at rest. God has forgiven me...

Ch'ol-Hun noted absolutely nothing about his own feelings on hearing that story, but I felt convinced that through what happened to Pastor Na he had been exposed to a powerful temptation urging him to mingle with people in the outside world, with people he did not know.

If that was so, had the Ch'ol-Hun who on February 18 became acquainted with both Pastor Na and Shin-Hyei cast off his shell of solitude? Had he struck up relationships with new friends at his workplace? And hadn't he felt obliged to change the subject of that *General's Beard* he intended to write? Hadn't he changed it so that the main character grew a beard like everybody else, then began to fight the beards?

I was anxious to know just how that psychological transformation had expressed itself in action. I even had the sudden feeling that I had fallen into a trap. I had the feeling that I ought to meet the man who had first introduced me to him. According to his diary, it had been June when he resigned from his job with the newspaper. The passages where he wrote about things that had happened at work mostly dealt with events occurring before he met Pastor Na. From February onward, almost every entry was either about Pastor Na or Shin-Hyei. I resolved to visit the newspaper offices on the following day.

6

It was my first visit to the newspaper since I finished the novel they had serialized. I thought they would have gone to press already but the editorial office was in an uproar. Telephones were ringing on all sides. The voices answering the phone all seemed to be yelling, pitched an octave higher than the surrounding din.

"Lee Ch'ong-Gil, twenty-two; Park Tok-Man, sixty; Kim Ok...Hee? What? Hui? H...u...i...ok; what did you say? Just six? Six years old?"

They seemed to be receiving lists of names by long-distance telephone from somewhere in the provinces. It looked as though there had been some kind of big accident.

Mister Kim was in the electrotype room. While I was waiting for him I went over and sprawled in the visitor's chair beside the chief editor's desk.

"Has something serious happened?"

"You can't have seen the special editions. People crushed in a stampede. Lots of people crowded into a cinema down south to see a visiting movie-star and it seems someone had the bright idea of shouting "Fire!" to clear some of them out. In the panic that followed...about twelve people were trampled to death."

I suddenly had a vision of flocks of wild animals, herds of elephants racing through some African forest away from a forest fire.

"Trampled to death?"

The incident had no bearing on it, of course, but in some weird way it conjured up in my mind Kim Ch'ol-Hun's death...an image of Kim Ch'ol-Hun being trampled to death by a herd of wild elephants. A newspaper office is always a busy place. Their real workplace is not this building; it's out where things are happening. They can never foretell where they will be at any given time. Was he really able to endure that kind of work? Yet he had deliberately chosen the job, hadn't he? Still, wasn't there something in Ch'ol-Hun's diary about how being a newspaper photographer had made him more lonely?

I thought about that passage as I smoked a cigarette.

I'm invariably standing behind the camera lens. There's no way I can dash out in front of the lens and enter the world that I'm photographing. I always have to be out of sight, keeping a proper distance from what's out in front.

I go running after events. I have to be out where the news is. But at the same time as I'm wherever the news is, I always have to stay out of the news. The camera reporter is not like the news reporter; he has no right to inquire about why something happened, or how it's turning out, or what the last word is. All he has to do is take the pictures, develop them, print them off, and hand them in at the desk. There are even times when it's only after reading the article accompanying some picture I took that I understand clearly what was happening out there.

My place is behind the lens, not in front. I'm sorry I quarreled with that reporter. He couldn't understand how I felt, and it was only natural. I couldn't stand the way he told me, "Just get your pictures taken and head straight back. I'm the one doing the reporting."

Of course my job was done once I'd snapped that suspect's face. But I couldn't simply carry on and ignore the fact that as the police were taking him away he shouted out to his daughter: "Suny, tell dad I'm innocent." I've taken photos of a lot of faces. Yet for the most part I never knew who they were.

Given the atmosphere in the editorial office, I could understand how Ch'ol-Hun must have felt. The editor seemed to have asked me something but I hadn't heard him, so I just replied, "Yes," dragging out the end in an ambiguous manner. I felt that I ought to ask him something in return. People like to feel you're interested in them.

"Kim Ch'ol-Hun's dead?"

The editor scratched his nose with the tip of his pen and stared toward his office.

"That was a long time ago."

It looked as if he were waiting for the finished copy for the last edition. He probably felt that a death that at least got a mention on the local page was more important than the death of Kim Ch'ol-Hun. The editor's attitude betrayed a trace of resentment. Yet this was someone he had lived with for more than a year as a member of his staff.

"They seem to suspect murder..."

At that, the editor frowned slightly.

"Who would have wanted to kill him? He had no money, and he was not someone anyone would notice particularly. He was out of a job and life must have been difficult."

He assumed that he had killed himself because life was difficult since he was unemployed. At the same time, he showed no sympathy.

"Because he was out of a job..."

I was taken aback to realize that there could be yet another viewpoint, considering unemployment as the reason for his death. There were countless reasons. Now "reason" may sound very scientific but I have discovered that in fact it is always employed as an ambiguous and subjective word. Mister Kim was coming toward me, wiping his glasses on his necktie.

"Why, what's up? It's good to see you again."

We exchanged the customary greetings, then went down to the company coffee-shop in the basement. Mister Kim is the younger brother of a friend of mine. We have known each other since he was in high school.

"You introduced Ch'ol-Hun to me, didn't you?"

"He's dead. Coal-gas poisoning."

"I know! Did you go to the house to pay your respects?"

"There was not one person in the whole office who knew where his house was. That's the kind of fellow he was."

"Surely there must be an address-list of employees?"

"He'd left the newspaper a long time before. What's up? Did he give you that, what was it? beard novel and ask you to get it published?"

Mr. Kim was using the same turn of phrase as when he was in high school. He looked rather weary as he spun an empty film spool round and round on one finger.

I started by asking why his colleagues had disliked Ch'ol-Hun and the reply proved to be very simple. He had the aloofness of a rural gentleman-scholar; he was hidebound in his activities; he was unsociable in his habits; and so on. To give you one example, he added. He was so selfish that he'd be using the darkroom at the busiest hours of the day and always taking his time without any thought for anyone else.

Mister Kim too had been looking at Ch'ol-Hun from the other side of the wall. They had graduated from the same art college. They were both photographers, working for the same paper, yet he had been nothing more than just another human being for him. There had been something in his diary about his work in the darkroom. He used to like the darkroom.

Once I'm in the darkroom I feel perfectly safe because I'm completely alone. It's the middle of the day—outside, the sunlight will be pouring down, with people swimming through its glare like so many fish. And I'm all on my own standing here like this in the darkroom, cut off and isolated from the light and sound and air of the outside world. In the thick darkness the fluorescent screen is casting a livid glow like a full moon. It looks like a doorway opening onto the world beyond.

The sharp tang of the hypo, the darkness, the glow, the purr of the timer with its phosphorescent hand turning.... Ah, this is Eternity! A Paradise of eternal sleep. Working in the darkroom liberates me.

"What's a fluorescent screen?"
Mister Kim laughed in a puzzled way at my sudden question.

"You're acting a bit oddly today, aren't you? Ah, I know! You're writing a novel and you've come in search of background. It must be hard writing novels. The fluorescent screen is something we use in the darkroom when we want to see a film's level of exposure...we can't use just any kind of light in a darkroom. In Hell there may be places where you find 'darkness visible,' but not in a darkroom. We need absolute darkness, which is why we use the fluorescent screen's special kind of luminosity—it's not really light at all. Just what it takes for us to see a film's degree of exposure...."

I did not want to take up too much time. Therefore I decided to ask just a few simple questions about some important points.

"From about February this year, wasn't there any change in his manner, especially in his attitude toward his friends?"

"Well, I don't know. I can't say exactly that it started in February, but in the time before he stopped working here, his attitude was certainly very odd."

He pointed his index finger toward his head and drew circles in the air; he meant to say he had lost his wits.

"What reason have you got to say that?"

I was furious, but Mister Kim said that he had been like that since college. While he was at art school, he had painted weird pictures, the kind of thing that are called abstracts now, and bewildered the professors.

"I want to paint realistic pictures too. But if you paint one thing, it means you're cutting off part of that thing; to save the one subject of your painting means eliminating many other objects all around it."

That was how Ch'ol-Hun stood up to his professors. According to Mister Kim, when they paint a landscape, it seems that artists cut off everything surrounding the view in order to paint that scene and nothing more, just like the square frame surrounding the picture. Ch'ol-Hun said that he hated that. He said he was worried about the scenery left over that didn't fit into the picture.

Besides, he said, if they were painting trees or houses, there were all kinds of things scattered round about them, stones or earth. But in order to concentrate on the subject they were painting, they would exclude all the other things. Ch'ol-Hun considered the artists' aesthetic intentions to be a form of violence against things. He said that he reckoned that each and every stone and pebble had a right to be there.

Therefore the other students used to make fun of him.

"Try taking photos of the landscape. Then it will come out exactly as it is, without anything being sacrificed."

Sure enough, the very next day Ch'ol-Hun turned up at school carrying a camera.

Then Mister Kim wanted to talk about the time he fought with Ambassador Kim.

"That habit he had of abruptly turning on people for no reason, like he did with Ambassador Kim."

"I've heard all about that."

I stopped him.

It seemed that the story of his quarrel with Ambassador Kim had become common knowledge in the newspaper office. He had described the incident in detail in his diary.

It had happened a few weeks before he met Pastor Na and the record of it in his diary constituted a unique piece of narrative, making a different impression and showing another aspect of Ch'ol-Hun.

It would have been much better if I had refused when that reporter from the political desk asked me to go with him to Ambassador Kim's house to take the photos for his interview. Naturally I was not tempted by his remark that if we went, we'd get a good meal. Ambassador Kim had spent not more than three years in the United States, yet he virtually spoke to us in English and at the end of every phrase he would pause and repeat, "Now how do you say that in Korean?"

His facial type was distinctively oriental. He had something of the Mongol about him, yet he harbored a smile imitating Ike's and he kept on shrugging his shoulders like a westerner. His wife, very excited, was all dressed up as if she were leaving for a party in five minutes. She was in such a state that if one of her ancestors of a century before had turned up in traditional dress and straw sandals, she would have killed herself in mortification. Still, I took it all in my stride.

"When I first came back to Korea, after taking my degree, that is.... My dear, the kimchi's so hot, it quite scorches one's stomach. Luckily tastes in food are not absolute. We really ought to start our reforms by changing the way we eat."

"When you first went to America," I blurted out, "how was it? Surely the butter was so greasy it scorched your stomach too?"

The reporter shot a sideways glare at me. Actually, the ambassador was the newspaper chairman's younger brother and we had been sent to write what is known in the newspaper world as an "in-house" article. I nonetheless continued to keep myself under control. When the time came to take the pictures, he made a great fuss about the gifts he said he had received in the United States, and arranged for them all to be in the background. He pointed out a picture showing him shaking hands with a certain high American dignitary.

"What do you think of that? It was taken by a photographer from the Washington Post...doesn't it make me look rather unnatural?"

I still controlled myself. My colleague spoke enthusiastically about how well American photographers get their camera angles, and even went so far as to commandeer it, proposing to publish it in the paper. Everything was going just fine until the time for the family photo. When the ambassador's wife called "Mary! Jim!" in the direction of the inner room, it finally happened. Hearing those names, I fully expected to see a couple of high class pedigree puppies emerge.

Then the door opened and I saw a pair of twins about four years old walk out. They were obviously not blond haired, but do you know, those kids were speaking English, calling out "Mummy, Mummy." The ambassador's wife (albeit as yet only a nominated ambassador's wife) perched one child on each knee and boasted proudly that so far they knew no Korean. Then mother and children began to chatter away ten to the dozen in an English from which the "t" sound had vanished.

My young companion looked curious. First he established the kids' ages, names, and relative English-speaking skills in his own rough English. Then gravely he proceeded to ask, "And do you like Mummy more, or Daddy?" as if he were reciting lines from one of Shakespeare's plays. Standing beside him, Ambassador Kim "translated" his English into his own fluent English for the children's benefit.

They replied that they liked their Daddy. Ambassador Kim glanced at me and explained, "That's the American way, you see. American kids generally prefer their father...." and again he flashed an Ike-like smile. I couldn't take it any more. Why did I get upset? Why was I not strong enough to stomach something that everyone else seemed prepared to take no notice of? I addressed a double bow to his wife and addressed her with the utmost civility.

"Excuse me, but don't those children have Korean names? Even if they still can't understand their own country's language, surely they must be able to recognize their own names. You may perhaps be unaware of the situation here in Korea. In our country, people use foreign names like Mary or Jim for dogs, bar-girls in dance-halls, or for foreigners' whores. Western things are all very well, but it's just western names that haven't been given a very high-class reception in our country so far. When I heard you calling your delightful offspring, I assumed you were calling your dogs. It's not the children's fault, of course, Madam."

The reporter swore at me first, then the ambassador's wife, and finally the dignified ambassador himself began to shout. If I'd only let it go at that, things might not have been so bad. But strangely enough, I could not control my agitation.

I burst out violently: "I don't want to sound moralizing, but I reckon it would be better to take one of the totem poles from the entrance to a village and send that as our ambassador, rather than a man like you."

If only I had not seen the ambassador's children, that day would probably not have witnessed such a disgraceful scene. I felt sorry for the kids. I reckoned that with no Korean and only dolls to play with, they could do nothing but watch other children playing from a distance, with hands behind their backs, like I used to when I was a child. I had the impression that they were undergoing my own sufferings. That was what I could not endure.

Since I knew all about the incident with Ambassador Kim, I told him to go on to what followed. Mister Kim expressed the opinion that it had not always been the case, but that at the time he left the newspaper he had definitely not been normal. He had put the empty film spool on the table and was rolling it about with the palm of his hand.

"That was surely the reason he left. He started to try to do things nobody had asked him to do. His eyes had a strange look about them, like someone haunted, and every time he saw any of us he would give us a broad smile. It was really weird. Then something happened. Do you know about that? There's this Yom Sang-Un, you see, the fellow who got last year's press-photography award...anyway, it involved Yom Sang-Un. His wife was dying of uterine cancer at the time. She would grasp hold of Yom Sang-Un's hand and refuse to let go. Yet at the same time, he couldn't spend every single minute stuck there with her...so he continued to go to work. Then one day he didn't go out to the scene on account of his wife, he just handed in a montage at the desk. A photo of the June monsoons, to go with an article revealing how the victims were sick and starving for lack of any proper policy toward them. It turned out that the photo he used was not a shot of an actual scene but one manufactured to fit the story. It was no great crime, but the investigating authorities got wind of it and came along. Low and behold Ch'ol-Hun started to swear blind that he was the one that had done it, instead of Yom Sang-Un. They arrested him. He made a simple problem into a complicated one, putting Yom Sang-Un and the newspaper in an awkward position. It was incomprehensible. There was that, and then he was asked to resign from the job."

"Did you think he was crazy?"

My face grew flushed. My voice grew louder. Mister Kim looked surprised; his hand stopped rolling the spool about.

"It was certain. And when he was asked to resign, there was a report from the psychiatric hospital. He was out of his mind."

I could understand him. Why had Ch'ol-Hun taken the blame for Yom Sang-Un's action? He must have sensed what that young woman would feel as she lay there, desperately sick, pursued by the fear of death. If Yom Sang-Un was arrested, she would surely lie awake, open-eyed, alone all that long night. He had felt that. He had considered that you couldn't tear away Yom Sang-Un's hand from hers, clinging so to speak to the last thread holding a dying life as it dangled above the void.

He had written nothing about that. Because he must have been afraid. That time he had knelt with his brother on the muddy ground by night in the pouring rain, begging his father to forgive him, trying to help him; or when Yi Jin had panicked trying to avoid the bullets and he had given up the sluice where he had taken cover, trying to save him... Every time he tried to do something for someone else, the result had been a monstrous failure.

He must have been eager to avoid going through that again. Human encounters were all mere chance, irrational, a thick layer of misunderstanding, and meaningless, like billiard balls freely rolling, bounding and rebounding. If he were forced to reach that conclusion once more, in the case of Yom Sang-Un, the pain would be very hard to endure.

It happened after Kim Ch'ol-Hun's meeting with Pastor Na and Shin-Hyei. It was a time when he was advancing step by step toward self-confidence, toward a new self-confidence that involved plunging deep into the thick of humanity.

I had a feeling that I ought to get out of there before I began to hate Mister Kim. Outside the coffee-shop, the paper had just been rushed off the press and there was the sound of boy's voices shouting raucously. The uproar was spreading in waves, farther and farther afield.

7

Under pressure from my publishers, I did not go out for a few days. I was determined to start writing. Not that I had forgotten Kim Ch'ol-Hun. I kept reading his diaries in spare moments. He had written about the sparrows perched on the wire fence and about scraps of food in the sewers, the early morning wind, the monsoon rains, the sound of the radio drifting in from next door, about laborers hanging from ropes cleaning the windows of high buildings, about vegetable salesmen and handcart men from the countryside—insignificant details in the world about him. The subject matter was all about ordinary, common-or-garden things, but they were not the kind of factual observations that you can easily find anywhere. Neither was it some kind of idealized fiction. Putting it briefly, it was reality grown abstract. I had the impression that I was reading a poem or looking at a picture by a surrealist.

What struck me was the way reality grew increasingly abstract with every page of the diary, so that by the time I reached his separation from Shin-Hyei I was finding it almost impossible to understand what he was writing. Occasionally, though very rarely, like when you wake from a dream or when fog lifts briefly, some vivid passages would occur, realistically treated, but they soon turned back into fantasy. Comparisons using "like" or "as" or "as if" faded into metaphors and finally even the metaphors were lost in a crowd of evocations that I could not interpret. They had become so utterly *déformé*.

There were innumerable riddle-like phrases such as "At the footbridge the wheels were falling off a horse cart," or "At my fingertips I could hear the sound of the wind sweeping through the forests of Sarawak," or "the porthole was smashed and salty sea water came pouring in so that it was impossible to go on listening to the music," and "I wonder why icy water troubles me."

Things concerning Shin-Hyei were equally transformed into fantasy. There was even a phrase to the effect that "I could no longer stand the sound of Shin-Hyei hacking away at her flesh." Yet something even harder to understand was the way that, from the day he and Shin-Hyei broke up until directly before he died, for almost a week the diary was suddenly written in a perfectly ordinary, normal narrative style. My head was aching so badly that I could no longer go on reading his notes.

It was just then that I received an unexpected phone call from Shin-Hyei. She spoke warmly, as if to an old friend.

She said that in the meantime she had become the object of new suspicions because of the camera and Inspector Park had been pestering her. Now everything had been cleared up and she wanted to talk with an untroubled heart, she was not even frightened that I might use it as the subject for a novel. That human voice, flowing from the receiver like a portion of Ch'ol-Hun's notes, made me aware of a wall. Shin-Hyei's voice flowing out from behind the wall....

I felt acutely the truth of the commonplace saying that "time is the best medicine." Shin-Hyei seemed to have cheered up. In order not to spoil her good humor, I agreed to meet her in the Sky-lounge of Bando Hotel. The evening would be best. It would be nice to talk looking down at the November city. We would meet at seven o'clock.

Shin-Hyei had arrived first and was sitting there. Dressed in a black leather jacket, Shin-Hyei looked fresh, like someone out hunting in the hills. Her warm eyes, flickering with black flames that looked as if they were about to melt something, were unchanged. Shin-Hyei dispensed with the usual formal opening greetings about the awful weather or my health and launched directly into what she wanted to say.

"Why are you so interested in someone dead? Aren't the living more important?"

"Certainly. You're alive, for a start. You're breathing and you can enjoy a drink. If you're bored you can yawn. So let's be interested in Shin-Hyei."

I nimbly eluded Shin-Hyei's question. She said she would have a Tom Collins. Because of the sky-lounge's blue-tinted windows, Seoul had a mysterious air, rather like a phosphorescent fish swimming in an aquarium. The evening was clear but chilly, one of those moments when the hiss of steam in the radiators makes you very snug.

"I feel as if I'd known you for a very long time. The first time we met, it was as if I were being reunited with someone I'd been separated from."

I felt a little uneasy, but I adopted a familiar style of address. I had the feeling that it would be all right.

"That's what he said too. Only today I've decided not to talk about him. It's a lovely evening. Sitting here with a drink, until a few minutes ago I could look down at Seoul, all squeezed into that space out there... Isn't it lovely?"

As she spoke, Shin-Hyei boldly thrust her bosom forward, as if she were practicing deep breathing. Cars' headlights cast great shadowy stains across the asphalt and vanished into the night.

"Shin-Hyei! We're not talking about Ch'ol-Hun. He's not here any more. When we talk about him, we're talking about ourselves. What you say is right, but this is for the sake of the living. We're drinking a toast in the glass that Ch'ol-Hun drank from and left behind. What I want to know is the reason why you and he separated, and whether he could really have died because of you."

A shadow once more fell over Shin-Hyei's face. She laid a hand across her breast. She seemed to touch the copper cross hanging at her neck.

"You know, that's what I keep asking myself. At first I found him strange and likeable, with that dreamy air of his. It was a time when I was tired of being surrounded by all those men stinking of the tripe they'd been eating. Besides, father had just died. People who are sad become a little unreal, don't they? He just called it 'inner light' and he was true to it. I made no secret of the fact that I liked him too."

"Immediately after your father died, you and he...in his lodgings..."

Shin-Hyei smiled sadly.

"You're having scruples again. Yes, that was the time we started to live together. I wonder why you have scruples about pronouncing the words 'live together.' Is it such a foul expression? Perhaps it is if you write the word in Chinese characters. On account of the character for 'live' especially, it makes you think of two wild beasts mingling their fur in a cave. Only we were no wolves or foxes. A pair of little squirrels perhaps, if you like. Anyway, our cohabiting was a far cry from anything like the life of animals up in the hills. 'In a cave' is right enough. It really was like being in a cave. But the animals in the cave were those mythical ones called *muoh* in the Chinese legends, that feed on people's dreams."

Waiters in white were carefully threading their way between the tables, as if passing down hospital corridors. The temperature indoors was agreeable.

"The sky-lounge gets dreary in autumn."

I was not going to let Shin-Hyei squirm her way out of trouble like that. I brought her attention back from the hairy fern she was staring at.

"Were you a *muoh* too?"

"At first. But from the start I had my mind firmly fixed on realities, those that smell of lard and dripping. That was where we differed. He was intent on beautifying his wounds and exchanging this world for an imaginary one; I was not. My wounds have made me more attentive to realities."

"From the moment you so melodramatically lost your virginity?"

I felt awkward saying that, but I pretended to be drunk to reduce the effect.

"Don't ask about precise details. Yet I can't deny the truth of what you say. At first I thought I would die. As I lay in the train listening to the sound of the wheels, gazing out at the wintry barley-field furrows speckled with snow, I thought of falling out and dying. But just as I was about to throw myself out, I felt something like a hot ball of fire rise into my throat. My whole being was ablaze with a desire to live—it was quite different from regret at leaving life behind—with a feeling that I had to live. Every time I have experienced difficult moments, the same ball of fire that I wanted to extinguish comes rising again. I don't know what it is. I can't say for sure. It was as if I were mad, or like a great gale; I simply wanted to live, passionately and intensely. Inside of me there was a fire, but the doors were firmly shut. Shut and locked fast. It was on the verge of exploding, like underground lava in search of a volcanic vent. I was trying to find someone who had the key that would open those scalding doors. I felt sure that if once, just once, I could find someone who would insert and turn the key, life would erupt and come bursting out, that the fire imprisoned inside me would kindle everything around me as it flowed freely outward."

The dark flames were flickering brightly in her eyes.

"You mean that Ch'ol-Hun didn't have that key either? That instead he only locked the door more tightly shut and fanned the fires burning inside?"

Shin-Hyei looked surprised and glad. She clapped her hands.

"Yes, yes, you've got it exactly. That's exactly what it was. There came a moment when I couldn't endure it any more. I had the feeling that if I didn't get away from him, I was going to end up so badly burned that I would have no choice but to die of it."

"Right! Now, Shin-Hyei, won't you play the confession game with me?"

I sat silently, ready to listen to what Shin-Hyei would say. I combined Ch'ol-Hun's incomplete and blurred diary pages, full of enigmatic riddles, with Shin-Hyei's vivid story, and a full picture of the life they had lived together began to appear clearly, as a drawing appears on a piece of magic paper or rather, like a colored photo emerging from a process printer.

Shin-Hyei's words gave bones to what was contained in Ch'ol-Hun's diary, while the contents of his diary fleshed out the bare bones of Shin-Hyei's tale. You might equally say that, if his diary was the negative film, Shin-Hyei's story was like a positive print. Once that unrecognizable negative was projected onto the print paper, the result seemed likely to be pretty close to the real picture. By combining both their viewpoints, I was able to weave together a single story in my mind.

Ch'ol-Hun termed his life together with Shin-Hyei "drifting" and called his rented room upstairs their cabin. He remarked to Shin-Hyei, "We're drifting endlessly onward. All the other passengers have already drowned. Waking here in this shattered cabin, we're the only two left, drifting onward." Sometimes he would remark, "We've been drifting for a month now," or if something good happened he would say, "For the first time since we've been adrift an island has appeared."

Ch'ol-Hun turned everything into fantasies of that kind when he spoke. Their activities together in bed he used to term "a purging of loneliness" or "a solitary assault" or "a fleshly dialogue" while his leaving for work at the newspaper office was called "going fishing."

"You just stay there and enjoy the sea breeze. I'll go and catch the fish we need for our supper. Won't you pass me my rod...?"

By his rod he meant, of course, his camera.

At first Shin-Hyei had enjoyed the game. She felt it was not like life at all, but like a play acted by little school-children. They would lean out of the "porthole" and feel utterly contented by a sunset or the spectacle of the filthy sea (the city landscape) with debris floating on it.

Their life's daily course was always the same. They played not only "the confession game" but also "chieftains." It was always Ch'ol-Hun who invented their pastimes.

He used to say that one day their drifting craft would reach a new continent not marked on any chart. He used to say that a phoenix would come flying up to them, or natives appear wearing nothing but banana leaves. He explained that they would be a primordial race, not recorded in the dictionary of human species, and their thoughts and deeds quite unlike those of the human beings we were familiar with.

One morning, in bright weather with a rustling breeze blowing as on a May-time dawn, he declared that they were arriving at the new continent. Ch'ol-Hun and Shin-Hyei would become the "chieftains," the masters of the new kingdom. That was what he meant by playing "chieftains."

"Will the noble chieftain not go hunting?" Shin-Hyei would ask and he would reply: "Not at all. The people here do not destroy life by such things as hunting. This is what you must say: Will the noble chieftain not go and feed the wild animals?"

Ch'ol-Hun was exactly like a small child. When he played, it was not just a joke; it was for real. Once Shin-Hyei asked, "Master, when shall we be going home again? This primitive life has grown boring. My head aches from all the perfumed essences these natives rub themselves with."

At this Ch'ol-Hun looked grave and gave vent to his anger.

"Shin-Hyei! Why, you're bored with playing chieftains? You think it's just a silly game? Why can't you understand? In this new continent we've discovered, the people know everything

LEE OYOUNG

a person is thinking without a word being spoken. They live constantly hand in hand, like in a round dance. They practice no deceit or disguise, no plotting or suspicion. No fences, no posts, no prisons, and without ever reading anything like a newspaper they live in perfect knowledge of one another. That's why our natives don't need to rub themselves with spices. And in their land absolutely nothing ever happens to give anyone a headache."

They spent most of their days playing either the chieftain game or the confession game.

Gradually Shin-Hyei began to feel uneasy. Ch'ol-Hun looked like someone sleep-walking or caught in a daydream, and it frightened her. She didn't feel tense when they were playing chieftains, but as soon as the confession game started she always felt gloomy. The harder Ch'ol-Hun tried to be forgiving and reconciling, the more he tormented himself in self-mortification and a nearly pathological desire to justify himself.

"Shin-Hyei! Why on earth do I do such things? On my way back to the office today, I knew perfectly well that all I had in my wallet was a ten-*won* note. Yet still, when it was time to pay the fare, I took out that ten-*won* note and held it up to the light as if I were afraid I was taking out a hundred-*won* note by mistake. I was just play-acting. It was all because I felt guilty and thought that the other passengers would laugh if they knew that I only had ten *won* in my wallet. Shin-Hyei! It was such a wretched performance. There was no one paying the slightest attention to me; no one was going to laugh on realizing that I only had ten *won*. Yet there I was, acting as if my wallet were stuffed full of banknotes. Why? I won't.... Shin-Hyei. I won't do such a thing again."

As a general rule, all his confession games followed the same pattern. If ever Shin-Hyei claimed that she had nothing

88

to confess, he would get cross and claim she was keeping some secret from him. That was the way they lived together. Then the summer rainy season came. There would be no sunlight for several days at a time. A sour mustiness filled the room while the ceiling and walls dripped with humidity. Heavy clouds, gray like rats' fur surged past the westward-looking window they had been calling their porthole. Shin-Hyei felt bored and listless.

She was listening to the splattering raindrops. She gazed down into the backyard, where as soon as one raindrop had flowed into the drain another followed. Suddenly a mass of flames rose into her throat while her breast began to burn fiercely. It was the first time it had happened since she met Ch'ol-Hun. From that day onward, Shin-Hyei was unable to quench the fire blazing inside her. The flames were licking across her crimson tongue in search of a volcanic vent. But the door was still firmly shut.

"Ah! I want to live. Not in some childish fantasy; I want to live in a proper reality, where blood comes flowing if I'm scratched."

Shin-Hyei examined the picture by Géricault hanging on Ch'ol-Hun's wall. It was the same picture she had always seen, yet somehow it looked quite different. It was a copy of the "Wreck of the Méduse" that showed seamen clinging to the stump of a broken mast and shouting. They were waving clothes they had stripped off toward the darkness and storm. The waves were towering high and the heavens were covered with clouds. In the face of those black waves that threatened to engulf their bronze-hued flesh, she beheld those shouting faces!

Shin-Hyei felt like throwing the window open and screaming into the rain-drenched space beyond.

"Rip open this door. I want to live. I really want to live, to live."

Ch'ol-Hun had stopped working. He never left her for a moment, but sat beside her all day long, like a shadow. For that reason she felt all the more like shouting something. She had tried to bring the fire to an eruption by "fleshly dialogue," but at those moments Ch'ol-Hun always looked at her with a fearful expression in his eyes. He would caress her physical body with a kind of animal's homing instinct, but then he would abruptly kick at the nest and go flying up into the empty expanses of somber imagination.

That evening, rain was still pouring down. When their "purging of loneliness" was over she roused herself from her despondent lethargy. Ch'ol-Hun had fallen into a weary doze.

"It's raining again! Out in the soaking wet fields the mice must be shaking their fur...that's what I'm like now."

Shin-Hyei had nothing to do. She began to cut her toenails. Suddenly Ch'ol-Hun shouted aloud like someone crying for help, "Ah! Don't make that sound. Stop cutting your nails."

He was blocking his ears with his hands. "He's in torment again." Shin-Hyei knew that it only had to rain for Ch'ol-Hun's sense of hearing to become extremely acute. She knew. She knew that his brother had kept shouting his name out into the rain-filled night as he was taken away. She stopped cutting her toenails. She tried to comfort Ch'ol-Hun, who was sitting up on the bed gazing at her face. She was thinking, "He can hear his rain-soaked brother's voice, that's what it is." But he spoke with a voice filled with regret as if he were playing confessions. It was not what she had thought.

"You must be bored. Listening to the rain and cutting your toenails.... Only I beg you not to do that. Else I'll end up despising you. I always considered your body to be like a fish as you lay there beside me after we had purged our loneliness. I had the impression that you were a different person. Fish drawn up on to dry land open and close their gills in search of water, don't they? I felt there was something fish-like about the way your shoulders move up and down as you breath. I had been intending not to tell you this, Shin-Hyei; it was wrong of me to let myself be reminded of a fish's flesh with all the scales gone. Will you scold me? Seeing you cutting your nails only made the impression stronger. Nails are a part of a person's body too, you see. Of course, since they have no sense of feeling, people can cut their nails without feeling any pain, as if they were sharpening a pencil. But when you cut your nails with that cracking sound, my mind feels pain as if bones were snapping, as if a nerve were being stabbed with a needle. I can't stand that sound. Is it because of the way the muggy night is fluttering lightly away? Forgive me, Shin-Hyei."

They both went out in search of work. Ch'ol-Hun said he would contribute nude photos to foreign photographic magazines, and Shin-Hyei said she would go back to the dance studio she had once frequented and get a job. For the first time, she began to feel that she had been wrong to drop out of school, back in the days when she had been working her way through a college course in physical education.

Things went on like that until the autumn. Confession games and chieftain games grew infrequent. At the same time, Ch'ol-Hun said he was writing a novel and talked a lot about it with Shin-Hyei.

It was *The General's Beard.*

"What do you think? Suppose I finally let the main character grow a beard. No, it'll be better if he ends up not growing one..."

Shin-Hyei made up her mind to leave him any number of times.

The rainy season was long past and it was late autumn. Shin-Hyei received a call from the police, to the effect that Ch'ol-Hun was there and they had some questions to ask her.

Ch'ol-Hun was sitting on an ancient creaky chair, staring at the posters on the police station walls. Shin-Hyei reassured the officer in charge as to Ch'ol-Hun's identity and answered a few questions.

"I assure you that he's not mentally disturbed."

The officer knitted his brow, which was of that narrow kind frequently found in people devoid of imagination. Shin-Hyei felt like a primary school student's mother summoned to meet her offspring's form-master. Ch'ol-Hun had gone to the kindergarten. Shin-Hyei knew that sometimes, when he had nothing else to do, Ch'ol-un would go to the kindergarten near the local ward office and watch the children play.

That day, Ch'ol-Hun had made trouble. The children were playing a game out in the yard. It was a game that you often see kindergarten children play. The teacher stands in the middle, clapping, while the children circle round in time to the rhythm. Then One, Two, Three, Four...the teacher calls out a number and the children run to form groups with that number in them. If it's Five, five to a group; if it's Three, three to a group. The children have to match off. It all has to be done very quickly, in the time it takes to count to three. No matter how quick they are, some of the children fail to match up in time and have to drop out. The last child left is the winner. Ch'ol-Hun had been watching them.

The children were shouting noisily as they ran about to form their groups. If a child tried to join a group that was already complete, the children chased it away. Otherwise the whole group would be "out." Ch'ol-Hun spotted one child that could not find a place anywhere, running about among the completed groups.

The teacher called out, "Anyone who can't fit in has to drop out. Off you go, now."

Ch'ol-Hun suddenly went rushing up to the teacher.

"Why are you making the children play that game?"

Ch'ol-Hun gave the teacher a push. The watchman came running up and took him to the police box.

"What normal person would ever do such a thing? Anyway, it looks as if he'll do dangerous things if he goes out. As his wife, you must take good care of him."

She had taken him back home.

I can't leave Ch'ol-Hun. He's a thirty-year-old child. He's sick and needs someone to look after him.

Shin-Hyei wavered in her resolve to escape from that cave, or rather from that aimlessly drifting ship's cabin.

It was true. He needed someone to look after him, a kind of substitute mother. Shin-Hyei had never believed him when he kept repeating that he would "be obliged to go down to the countryside and farm with Mother." "He'll just go on drifting. He'll keep on and on drifting, clinging to a drifting hull. He's clinging to me, after all." Shin-Hyei reflected that she could not let go of that clinging hand.

Thereupon the fateful day arrived. After a long interval, Ch'ol-Hun suggested they play the confession game. It was the evening before they split up. Winter was coming. The window was rattling and the wind was blowing with a whistling noise. They had for the first time done some shopping that day. Shin-Hyei had found a job in that estate agents office and on the first day had taken an advance on her wages, as they were going to have to buy a coal-briquette stove. It was only a vulgar stove, but it was the first purchase they had made since they had been living together.

They lit the stove, and basked in its warmth, feeling as if they were camping up in a wintry mountain refuge. They listened to the wind. Suddenly Ch'ol-Hun proposed that they play confessions. He took his turn first.

"Shin-Hyei, do you realize that my camera's gone? I gave it to the model who poses for my nude photos. I've decided not to take any more pictures."

For the first time, sitting there in front of him listening to his confession, Shin-Hyei was shocked.

"As she was leaving the studio she said she was going to have a cup of tea and I went with her. What she told me touched me deeply. She's originally from a wealthy family and until last year she had a private car take her to school. Only then there was the coup, her father was put into prison for political reasons. She's an art student, that's why she took up nude modeling to earn her school fees. How do you think she felt when she first took off her clothes in front of people? You know how even a fallen woman hates letting any man see her body. And she had to take off her clothes and reveal her pale flesh in broad daylight. To think that she does it to earn a living; it's enough to make you weep. She told me, 'It was the reverse; for me it was the other way around. Before ever knowing a man, I lost all sense of shame about my body.' She clenched her teeth and spoke with conviction. Now I'm a corpse. A breathing corpse, or if not that, some kind of object. Because my hands, my breasts, and my limbs have all lost their original purpose. The mouth is for eating and talking; the breast for breathing; the legs for walking; the hands for smoothing the hair or carrying a handbag. But a model only uses those things for show, so much useless flesh, nothing but a faint shadow, a few curves, some bumps, a line, just an outline, a volume. It's with thoughts like those that she removed her clothing item by item and climbed up to pose on the modeling stand.... The day we met, it was her mother's birthday. Her mother had been selling off her personal trinkets as if she had no other goal in life. Right on down to the last one, her wedding ring. On learning of that, she asked the jeweler not to sell it. She told me that she wanted to buy it back and take it home as her birthday present. Only she had no money..."

Ch'ol-Hun had given her his camera. He stopped and asked Shin-Hyei to confess something too. He used to make an angry scene if she said she had nothing to confess. Shin-Hyei made up her mind; she began to confess. For the one and only time, she really felt disgusted with Ch'ol-Hun.

"I'm fed up with it. I'm making my last confession. If you think I'm jealous of what you did for that girl, you're making a big mistake. It's something I decided a long time back, right back in the summer rains. I'm sick and tired of chieftain games and confession games; even imagining that novel sickens me now. This is no 'Doll's House'; it's a 'House of Fables' or a 'Hollow Room.' I've got to get out of here. You're all the time talking about wounds, wounds...wounds...but what about all the rest, the parts that haven't got wounded? There's a lot more of them, and they're more important. Even if your whole being is wounded, it's nothing compared with the whole of life. I've decided to move out of this room tomorrow."

Ch'ol-Hun took it for jealousy over the model. He simply kept begging her not to misunderstand.

"You're nothing but a ruined aristocrat."

Shin-Hyei said his sympathy was extravagant.

The next morning, Shin-Hyei was getting her things together. Ch'ol-Hun made no attempt to dissuade her; he just stood there and watched her pack.

"Why don't you try to dissuade me?" Shin-Hyei asked.

"You really meant it...but I reckon you'd better go. I realized that while you were packing...that we're just like everybody else, I mean. I used to think that I was experiencing a miracle, two bodies becoming one. We spent a whole six months together. Yet watching you pack, I see that your things and my

things are strictly and systematically distinct, that they have
been here from the very start as different people's things.
Watching you bundling up your luggage, I realized that your
things and mine were perfectly unmingled and could be
separated remarkably easily. Now this toothbrush is yours. This
mirror, too. This sock is mine, and this book is mine, this fountain-
pen is yours..."

Ch'ol-Hun spoke as if screaming in despair. Still watching,
as Shin-Hyei put her seamless stockings into her suitcase, he
went on.

"And those socks. From the very beginning, the unique things
that I always saw as belonging to someone else were your
socks. Do you know what I used to be looking at when you got
into my bed? Those socks, fluttering down on the floor like a
cast-off skin. Another person's things...that's what I used to
murmur to myself as I looked at them."

Shin-Hyei did up her bag, sat on the bed and hugged Ch'ol-
Hun.

"We're people who were destined to part some day. Write
your novel. That way you can make your imaginary world come
true, and you'll be more at ease. I'm just one of those people
with their too solid flesh, simply another mammal, nothing more.
I don't know how to metamorphose like a silkworm. It's true
you have to write your novel. So I'll listen one last time. How
does your novel end? I suppose the hero decides not to grow a
beard?"

Ch'ol-Hun was gently biting his lip.

"All right! I'll write my novel. This time I won't repeat the
old tragedy where helping somebody results in their getting
hurt. Because so far all the people I've liked have ended up
getting done in! I can't possibly want you to end up like that.
I've been sweating over the question of how *The General's*

Beard ends for ages now. But watching you leave, I've got an idea that I think I can use."

"Won't you tell me?" Shin-Hyei asked eagerly.

Ch'ol-Hun began to speak, "*The General's Beard* ends one rainy summer's day..."

Drizzle was falling through the foggy air. He was crossing the road by an overpass. A beetle, a squashed black beetle was dying there, floating like a scrap of fluff. He walked on, avoiding the beetle. Beards, rain-soaked beards were pursuing him. He tried turning into a dark alley-way, escaping from the beards. But now a black jeep, a black jeep with its number-plate covered, had him in its headlights and was hurtling after him.

The driver's face was covered by a general's beard. He tried to escape. But the jeep followed him, making a sharp turn into the alley. He lifted a hand, trying to escape from the dazzling headlights. He heard a noise. There was a screaming of brakes. He was falling, struck by a mass of beards. It was raining. Thick fog. The jeep's headlights vanished into the night.

He turned his head toward the vanishing lights.

"I'm dying because of a beard. I've been murdered. Ah— the last man not to grow a beard is dying. I am the one person who did not change, the unique person to preserve intact the human face as it was before beards were worn. But they will say it was a traffic accident. A chance traffic accident."

He was dying. No one was watching over his body. He saw another layer of darkness covering the night. In that darkness kindergarten children were walking toward him; it was as if he were watching a silent film.

He could hear nothing, yet they seemed to be singing and playing some kind of game as they approached him. All the children were wearing beards, general's beards, as if they were acting in a school play. He could feel those children with their beards drawing closer, their gestures soundless as in an old silent film. He died.

After she had heard the end of the novel, Shin-Hyei stood up. Outside, winter was coming. Carrying her suitcase, she emerged from the narrow alley. She hurried out of the alley, littered with the frozen bodies of rats. Ch'ol-Hun must be looking out after me from the porthole. He's drifting on alone now.

Shin-Hyei laughed sadly. She walked on toward the city streets with their stench of tripe, footsteps clattering like so many typewriters, drunks staggering, and cars racing.

"Do you think he died because of me?"

Shin-Hyei lifted the red cherry from her Tom Collins and placed it in her mouth. She then stared into my face, looking anxious.

"I told Inspector Park that I would find out the cause of his death. And yet.... I'm not sure. There's no easy explanation. There's something vaguely there but I can't explain it. Now it's all over."

I meant it. I could plainly call to mind the face of that person called Ch'ol-Hun. I could feel I had been his closest friend, but I had no right to speak about his death.

"A sky-lounge in winter is a gloomy place."

Shin-Hyei glanced around. It was time to go. We were the only people left, surrounded by empty chairs.

8

I finally managed to finish my manuscript for the publishers. It was later than promised, but at last I was free to leave Savannah Hotel. It was December 23rd; tomorrow would be Christmas Eve. I reflected that I ought to buy presents for my relatives down in the country. I had no further curiosity concerning Kim Ch'ol-Hun. My meeting a few days previously with the psychiatrist had been my last effort in the attempt to discover the reasons for Kim Ch'ol-Hun's death. Doctor Yun had spoken of "the Seventh Veil."

"There's the seventh veil. There was a film about it, you remember. Everyone is wearing seven different veils as they go about their lives surrounded by other people. We live solidly disguised. Then as we grow close to someone else, the veils are stripped off one after another. But we can never remove more than the fifth veil. There remains the veil that we can only remove when we are alone with ourselves, and the veil that we ourselves do not know. Removing the seventh veil, that veil of the heart, is the task of the psychoanalyst. You are making a big mistake if you think that you can uncover the reason for someone's death by reading their diary or listening to the things they say. To find out the reasons for a person's death, you have to look into their unconscious mind, the gulf of the unconscious that they too knew nothing of, the seventh veil; only then is an explanation possible."

According to Doctor Yun, Ch'ol-Hun was suffering from an Oedipus Complex. That was clear just from his novel about "the general's beard." Analyzed according to the psychology of the unconscious, the beard must represent the father, meaning authority. The fact that he was unable to weep when his father died should also be seen as a sign of the Oedipus Complex.

He explained how, once he was deprived of that controlling power, a split personality had developed. Shin-Hyei had been a substitute mother for him but when he heard that his real mother was coming up from the countryside, a conflict had arisen between the two images. He felt certain that in his unconscious Ch'ol-Hun had so to speak killed himself by fits and starts...

I felt no wish to hear anything more from Doctor Yun. It might be as what he said. But could there really be a formula that allowed you to explain someone's death as easily as solving a mathematical problem? I felt sorry for Doctor Yun. His was yet another viewpoint, merely adding one more complication.

I went out into the street. Santa Claus and his reindeer and white snow made of cotton-wool had a soothing effect. Poinsettias and cyclamens were blossoming behind greenhouse-like shop windows. Wave after wave of people bearing armfuls of gaily wrapped Christmas presents came flooding by. From the record shops came bellowing the sound of Christmas carols.

I turned into the streets around Myong-dong. There I suddenly glimpsed Inspector Park, wearing a ski-hat. He seemed glad to see me. He said that the Christmas season was always a busy one with the need for special anti-crime measures, but he looked perfectly relaxed.

We went into a little curbside grog-house, although it was still early.

"How's it going with the camera? Will you soon be arresting the criminal?"

I spoke with a pleasant sense of provocation. Inspector Park did not know what had happened to the camera, while I did. I felt the truly diabolical pleasure there can be in keeping a secret from another person.

"No problem. The statute of limitation on prosecution has a long time to run yet. There's still almost five years. I'll get the criminal in the end. Then I'll buy you another drink."

As time went by, the bar grew noisier. There were some who were already at the rowdy stage and were quarrelling in loud tones.

"No, hold on there...look...you've got it wrong, old friend. I ask you now: ish it posshible? Ol' pal...you've got it all wrong."

"And have you found the reason for his death? Have you caught the criminal responsible for his suicide? The one you said we would never be able to lock up? Why did he kill himself?

For what reason? Why did he die? Because he'd been fired? Because he'd been jilted? Because he was tired of living? Because he was crazy? Or because he couldn't get his novel written?"

Inspector Park laughed. He was beginning to get drunk. I was not feeling intoxicated.

"Because you have this statute of limitation on prosecution, at least once the date is past you can relax. Not that anyone ever keeps waiting that long anyway, surely? Whereas my investigation can never be complete, not until the day I die and not even then, not until my sons die and my sons' sons in the time to come. There is no statute of limitation on the search for the reasons of a suicide."

Inspector Park flicked on his gas-lighter and applied the flame to my cigarette. The cigarette I was smoking had gone out.

"Because I don't know him. Why, I couldn't even remember his name. It was only when you said he had been a photographer for that newspaper that I recognized him! So how can I know anything about his death? He died his own death. After all, nobody can explain another person's death. Each one of us is the only person who knows about his own death. I was wrong to think that I could explain another person's death. I have no right to know. But now I think of it, isn't tomorrow the day Jesus was born? You have to rejoice. People have to lift their glasses high. Won't you drink a toast? Not to death but to life...to someone being born, to that Birth. Here. Cheers to life being born...to the birth of Jesus and to our own kids' birth."

All of a sudden, drunkenness overwhelmed me. I wanted to go on and on chattering. I felt like talking about anything and everything with Inspector Park for a long, long time. I was so drunk that I felt inclined to recite in a loud voice some lines from that poem by Bishop King:

Stay for me there; I will not fail
To meet thee in that hollow vale.
And think not much of my delay;
I am already on the way.

Meanwhile the loudspeaker on the pavement in front of the bakery across the street was bellowing out a Christmas song:

"Tonight old Santa Claus
With his white hair, white beard,
Is coming on the wings of the wind."

Inside my head, other lines from Bishop King's poem overlapped with that:

And follow thee with all the speed
Desire can make, or sorrows breed.
Each minute is a short degree,
And every hour a step toward thee.

"Wearing his bright red hat,
His scarlet cloak wound round about him,
Through a cold land's snow he comes."

At night when I betake to rest,
Next morn I rise nearer my west
Of life, almost by eight hours' sail.
Than when sleep breathed his drowsy gale.

But hark! my pulse like a soft drum
Beats my approach...

THE GENERAL'S BEARD

I heard the sound of our glasses striking together as I sank into the surrounding uproar.

Phantom Legs

A personal re-reading of Stendhal's *Vanina Vanini*

Translator's Note: The portions of Stendhal's *Vanina Vanini* included in this work have been translated from the original French by the translator.

S a-Mi laid her nineteenth-century French literature textbook on the desk, with the thought that this was going to be the last test of her final examinations. The cover had faded to a dull yellow, and the title, *Vanina Vanini* in capital letters, could barely be read through the inkblots and scribbles that filled the empty space around it. Only faint traces remained of the long subtitle printed in small letters, *Particularités sur la dernière vente de carbonari découverte dans les Etats du Pape*, which were virtually illegible.

Sa-Mi had the impression that the picture of her sitting here studying for her last exam was already something that belonged to the past. She even ventured to wonder, rather unfairly, whether M. Stendhal, Henri Beyle, dead and buried these hundred years and more, could ever have imagined that one day far to the east, beyond countless lofty mountain ranges and prairies vast as oceans, a young woman would be spending a sleepless night on his account, preparing an examination.

It was a December night, one of those nights when people rub their hands and think of home, no matter how much work there is to be done. They cross snow-covered squares to drink a cup of piping hot black coffee in a café to the sound of steam rattling in the pipes. They dream of taking a train, a winter train, its roof all covered with snow as it rolls into the station in a flurry of swirling clouds of white steam; they dream of escaping from home, from the streets, from all that composes their inevitable destiny. Yes, it was the kind of winter night that somehow suggests such thoughts. Yet in the first lines of her copy of *Vanina Vanini* it was late one spring evening in nineteenth century Rome. A spring evening where the sound of carriages speeding, their lanterns swinging, down stone-paved streets toward nocturnal revelries, set people's hearts racing. Sa-Mi began to read the words of her text in a subdued murmur.

C'était un soir du printemps de 182*. It was one evening in the spring of 182*. All Rome was on the move, for His Lordship, the Duke of B****, the celebrated banker, was giving a ball in his new palace on the Piazza Venezia. All the greatest magnificence that could be produced by the arts of Italy, all the luxury of Paris and London, had been brought together to adorn this palace. A great crowd was flocking in. All the modest fair-haired beauties of noble England had sought the honor of being present at this ball; they arrived in droves. The loveliest women in Rome rivaled with them as to who was the most beautiful. A young woman, whose flashing eyes and ebony hair proclaimed her to be a Roman, entered on her father's arm; all eyes followed her. A singular degree of pride shone in her every movement.

One could see foreign visitors entering, astounded by the magnificence of the ball. "There is not one of the kings of Europe," they said, "whose festivities come near to equaling this."

Kings do not have a palace in the Roman style. They are obliged to invite the great ladies of their court while His Lordship, the Duke of B**** only summons beautiful women. On that evening he had been particularly fortunate in his invitations; the menfolk seemed dazzled. Amidst so many exceptional women some tried to determine which was the most beautiful. For a while the choice was unsure *but at last the princess Vanina Vanini, that same young woman with the black hair and blazing eyes, was declared the queen of the ball. Immediately the foreigners and the young Romans, deserting all the other rooms, crowded into the salon where she was to be found.*

"Why, there are still students incapable of reading figures in French!" Professor K exclaimed in tones of exaggerated surprise, as if he had just discovered something astonishing. "What in the world have you been doing these last four years? Of course, with all those demonstrations, there was no time left for you to study, but still.... And this is your final semester, *votre dernière classe*; surely you learned that in intermediate French? Your last class, *votre dernière classe*. You really only have to make a modicum of effort. 182* indicates an unspecified year, so when you read it in French you have to say *mil huit cent vingt et quelques*...the asterisk has to be read as *et quelques*."

"Right! Next, *tout Rome*...all Rome was on the move. Here *tout* signifies the whole...all the citizenry...all the citizens of Rome...Rome may be a feminine noun, so you must be careful to say, not *toute* but simply *tout*. All Rome was on the move, in uproar...." Seoul, all Seoul was in uproar. Spring 1960, a springtime evening in 182*... Rome, Seoul...April 1960. It was April. The cherry-trees were in blossom. Yet I did not need to use any skill to gain the honor of attending the masquerade. The citizens of nineteenth-century Rome were flocking toward the newly-built palace of the Duke of B*** on the Piazza Venezia to attend a masquerade given by the brilliant aristocrat. "*Concours*...signifies that the whole crowd was surging toward a single point. Later the sense changed and as it often came to be used to designate a large gathering, it acquired the sense of a 'competition.'" Only this was in Seoul. The demonstrators were surging toward the City Hall Plaza, not the Piazza Venezia. *Concours*...demonstration.... The party was the Last Supper for the men in power, the masquerade belonged to the demonstrators who were charging forward in a tight scrum.

The demonstrators were surging toward the presidential mansion, not toward a ballroom in the newly-built palace of the Duke of B***. *Les beautés blondes*, the fair-haired beauties, women in evening gowns, were passing like shadows down corridors of shining marble. That looks like a painting by Botticelli on that wall...and ah, the music! What music would it have been? In Rome one evening in springtime, melodies that went spreading endlessly, on and on through the gentle humid air. Toward people's hearts, and clothes, and windows, and then onward to the trees and fountains whispering out there in the darkness beyond...but our ball, Seoul's April 1960 springtime ball, was nothing like that. There was a sound of gunfire. The windows along the roadside were firmly shut, and the broad asphalt streets were deserted although it was broad daylight. There were no long marble corridors. There was no ballroom adorned with paintings by Botticelli. There were mounted troops blocking the way ahead. There was asphalt, and the pale green leaves just beginning to sprout on the roadside plane trees. Bathed in sweat, the students were bunched in a tight scrum, as they shouted and ran, running with hoarse cries.... This was our first ball. Someone was waving a flag. Students on a jeep were making signs, waving blood-stained, tattered shirts. They were shouting: we were to gather somewhere. They were shouting: we were to start something again. There was a crackling sound. Tear-gas canisters showered down like fireworks. "All the modest fair-haired beauties of noble England had sought (*avaient brigué*) the honor of being present at this ball...as you see, since they did their seeking (*briguer*) on the day preceding the ball, the verb is in the past perfect tense."

Only I had not at all sought to be present at this ball; it was simply because I had tamely obeyed my mother. I played the role of a spectator at the ball, sitting quietly upstairs at home like a potted plant on a terrace bright with begonias. At the sound of gunfire, mother had told me to close the windows, but I simply stayed sitting there gazing out at the crowd as it fell and rose, fell and rose, surging backward and forward like foam-crested waves. It was my first ball and my youth was growing to maturity in that ballroom.

Sa-Mi opened the window to refresh her addled thoughts. It was a night without light or sounds. On the screen during some movie white-gowned doctors had been excising the vocal chords of dogs in an experiment. Gobs of blood welling up...deprived of their voices, the dogs had nothing left but movements of pain. Without a voice, there is no way of indicating pain.

The night was writhing soundlessly, like those dogs deprived of their vocal chords. The still silence and darkness were devoid of all expression. The December night was drooping away like one of those dogs with its vocal chords excised. It had not been false to say, as Hyon-Su had done, that when there is neither light nor sound all things are suddenly deprived of existence. The darkness was gradually engulfing all the lights and sounds.

Her father, the prince don Asdrubale Vanini, desired her first to dance with two or three German rulers. After that she accepted the invitations of some very handsome and very noble Englishmen; their stiffness bored her. She seemed to find more pleasure in tormenting the young Livio Savelli who appeared to be deeply in love. He was the most brilliant youth in Rome, and a prince into the bargain; but if you were to give him a novel to read he would be sure to

*throw it aside after twenty pages, saying it gave him a
headache. In the eyes of Vanina, that was a disadvantage.*

*Around midnight a report spread through the assembled
dancers that made a considerable impression. A young
carbonaro, imprisoned in the Castello Sant'Angelo, had
just escaped, that very evening, thanks to a disguise; and
by a surfeit of romantic daring, arriving at the prison's last
guard-post he had attacked the soldiers with a dagger. Only
he too had been wounded, the constables were pursuing
him through the streets by the traces of blood he had left,
and it was hoped he would be recaptured.*

"There are men like Livio Savelli all over the world; call
them by an Italian name or by an English name, by a Mongolian
or an African or some barbaric name, it makes no difference.
They are people who never love truly, they are satisfied if they
are able to charm women. They only make love because they
are eager to test their own charm. People like Livio Savelli."
For no apparent reason, Professor K seemed to be growing
excited; as he went rattling on he began to introduce French-
style nasal sounds into his Korean. "Saying of this fellow that
'if you were to give him a novel he would throw it aside after
reading twenty pages' is as much as to say that he was lacking
in imagination. Yet as a general rule such fellows go up in the
world, don't they? Why, they have only to earn money, get a
pretty girl, and sit in a swivel chair signing things, and happiness
comes pouring in like interest on a bank account."

The Professor paused briefly and observed the reaction,
with an expression that suggested he was expecting them to
laugh. Students usually pretend to laugh at things they do not
really feel like laughing at. Otherwise the person trying to be
funny will feel put down. Prince Livio Savelli, now. That brilliant,
in all of Rome *le plus* the superlative, the most outstandingly

dazzling youth: supposing he had been sitting in that classroom, he would surely have laughed. Else the Professor might feel put down. "We seem to have slipped into gossip; *si on lui eût donné à lire un roman* if you were to give him a novel to read: this is the second form of the past conditional. Now surely, after a conditional *si* it is more normal to use the imperfect or the past perfect, is it not? Yet in cases such as this..."

Don Livio Savelli; the second form of the past conditional; the dark prison cells of Sant'Angelo; and did things like Don Livio Savelli and the second form of the past conditional exist in the prison of Sant'Angelo? Livio Savelli only shone with that superlative *le plus*. There could be no darkness for him. But between the dark towering mass of Sant'Angelo, and the starlight, and the ever tawny waters of the Tiber there is always the sorrowful sound of some aria echoing.

People were still telling one another this anecdote when, dazzled by the grace and the success of Vanina, with whom he had just been dancing, don Livio Savelli asked as he escorted her to her place, almost maddened by love:

"Tell me, I beg of you, who might hope to please you?"

"That young carbonaro who has just escaped," replied Vanina, "for at least he has done something more than merely bother to be born."

"I wanted to listen to some music..."

It was Sok-Hun who had rung at the door. Livio Savelli. I really don't understand why Father keeps wanting me to marry someone like him. I suppose it's because he's the youth in Seoul with *le plus* the superlative. Livio Savelli Kim Sok-Hun. Yet I've always thought that the only thing he had to show was the oil plastered on his hair. I don't know how many pages he would be able to read, if you gave him a novel. In any case, a week or so later there he would be, ringing at the door again holding the book, the novel he'd borrowed, making it his excuse. One short ring, one long, ever so casually. Then he'd say, "These novels are nothing much. I read them all to the end but the conclusion's always the same. After regrets, and hesitations, and people going astray, what do you get? Some kind of conclusion. Or rather the pretence of getting one, surely? What's the point of undergoing all those sufferings in order to arrive at such a meager conclusion? I really cannot endure these so-called authors; they're so pathetic. I mean, they're as stupid as mountaineers who sweat buckets climbing mountains they're going to have to come back down again. Why on earth climb a mountain in the first place when you're going to come down again?"

Sok-Hun was the kind of fellow to make remarks like that.

"I wanted to listen to some music..."

"You take our house for a public music room?"

"With the streets as they are, there's not even a tea room open with music worth listening to."

"What about taking part in the demonstrations, then?"

I've always wanted to embarrass him.

"I have no respect for such things. If I had that degree of ardor, I'd write you letters. The world gets not the least bit better because people bellow. It simply gets noisier. I know what people's courage is worth. Maybe you'll take me for a coward. Those others wave placards, then covered in blood and sweat they attack police cars that go careering about with sirens wailing, they get beaten with cudgels, dragged away like dogs.... So you wonder what sort of a person I am. Ringing doorbells and asking to listen to some music just in order to meet a girl. But that's all there is to it. It's just a matter of different kinds of courage. It doesn't matter which direction people run in, the earth keeps turning in the same direction. We might as well stay sitting down. Because whether we run or sit, the earth is still going to complete one revolution in exactly twenty-four hours. Do you realize how far around I've had to walk to get here? All the streets were blocked and the tear-gas was so thick I couldn't keep my eyes open. It wasn't all that easy for me to come here, either. It took courage, too. But let me tell you a secret. Observing the demonstrators I noticed that the farther back in the throng they were, the braver they were. And girl students holed up in their rooms like you are the bravest of all. Those who call people like me cowards are the ones hiding in a corner of their rooms. The demonstrators in the front row were terrified. You could see they were longing to turn and run; only their comrades behind were watching them and that's why they kept marching forward. Once you pass twenty, you live your life on the basis of what people will think. What people will think.... The demonstrators in the middle of the press, not those directly confronting the riot police, were wavering, hesitating whether to advance, but those at the very back were shouting at them to hurry up and charge. There weren't brave people, cowardly people, and hesitant people in that crowd. It was purely a matter of where one stood."

"While you weren't part of the crowd at all."

Professor K wrote *Mais* on the blackboard as he spoke.

"In cases such as this, *Mais* does not signify a direct contradiction or exclusion, it simply serves to link what follows with the preceding sentence. That is to say that '*Mais, de grâce, qui donc pourrait vous plaire?*' should be translated as 'Tell me, I beg of you, who might hope to please you?' To which Vanina replies 'That young carbonaro who has just escaped,' and finally explains that it is because 'at least he has done something more than merely bother to be born.'"

Sok-Hun spoke out.

"You mean that by joining the demonstration I might win your love? It would be a futile act. But even if everyone makes those same futile gestures, even if everyone takes the road leading to Hyoja-dong rather than demonstrate in front of the presidential mansion, I would always, always choose to be in front of your house, in front of your firmly closed front door, ringing the bell."

"*Ce jeune carbonaro*! I explained before, did I not, about *carbonaro*? *Carbonari* in the plural, *carbonaro* in the singular, is the name that was given to the members of a celebrated secret society in Italy that opposed the tyranny of Austria. They stood for liberal ideas and Italian unity. Just to make a digression."

Professor K gained in popularity by such digressions. He put on an expression as if to say, "I can't stop myself chattering away like this," but in fact he seemed to take a great deal of trouble to display his own culture and wit by those interruptions.

"Just a digression; but it makes one aware of an inconsistency *ironique*, very *ironique*. The *carbonaro*, who took the highest interest in things political and concrete, lived on the contrary highly sequestered lives, removed in the farthest degree from politics and concrete realities, as charcoal-burners, earning their living making charcoal deep in the mountains. Every form of disguise is similarly *ironique*. You remember how in one of Aesop's fables the lion is disguised as a fox? He's not mistaken. Is the fox going to disguise himself as a fox? So, is it not the same when our hero, this young charcoal-burner who has escaped from the prison of Sant'Angelo, disguises himself in female clothing? This brave fellow, brave enough to have stabbed a sentry with his dagger, dressed as a woman that trembles at the mere sight of a spider, is the lion disguised as a fox, isn't he? I know all this is only a digression but—how shall I put it?—surely, life is a kind of endless struggle where one is striving to put on a disguise and one is striving to remove a disguise. Only that the person wearing the mask and the person intent on removing the mask are not two distinct persons. Each one of us is wearing a mask and at the same time striving to remove every one else's mask. Generally speaking that's the kind of fight it is."

Sa-Mi addressed Sok-Hun:

"I still think that it's far more worthwhile for a person to be out shouting in the streets, even if it's pointless, than to be peeping into a girl's room. Because for them it's not enough to have been born in this world; they're after something more.

"Well of course. Obviously they're after something more. Like love, I mean. And money and getting ahead. Only here they are, already twenty, and they don't feel so sure about it any more. They're not upset about other people but about themselves.

"That's what I think. It was April, lovely April, and they had nowhere to go. Isn't this a time when it's hard to be satisfied with quietly watching the flowers bloom? Perhaps what they were after was actually something completely different. Something utterly different, something calmer and deeper, a room with a record player, with green curtains that are invariably gorgeous, a sofa to rest on, and some slightly difficult books to satisfy their vanity, a room like yours, so deep and calm. Perhaps that was what they really wanted."

Prince don Asdrubale came toward his daughter. He is a rich man who for the last twenty years has taken no heed of his steward, who lends him his own income at a very high rate of interest. If you meet him in the street, you would take him for an old comic actor; you would not notice that his hands are loaded with five or six heavy rings set with immense diamonds. His two sons entered the Jesuits and later died insane. He has forgotten them; but he is vexed that his only daughter, Vanina, refuses to marry. She is already nineteen and has rejected the most brilliant matches. For what reason? The same as that given by Sylla for abdicating: "scorn for the people of Rome."

Vanina refused the most brilliant matches out of "scorn for the people of Rome," but what can be the reason that I have so obstinately refused to marry Sok-Hun? "Scorn for doctors," perhaps? It's true he's a student in medicine. Oh yes. He's exactly the kind of man my father's looking for. After all, what he's after is not a husband for his daughter but a successor he can bequeath his hospital to. Someone to inherit it just as it is, right down to the signboard. Father has always insisted that even after his death the hospital must continue to be known as the Choi Ho-Un Surgery. Kim Sok-Hun would make a quite admirable head of the Choi Ho-Un Surgery. He's the kind of man who believes that the world goes on turning in its daily rotation even when he's quietly sitting down. Kim Sok-Hun would think it very natural to become another Choi Ho-Un. A tadpole feels no pain when it looses its tail. Father is hunting for a tadpole like that, poking away in messy, muddy water. He's no comic actor like Vanini's father don Asdrubale, getting into ever deeper debt with his servants and walking about with five or six great diamond rings on his fingers. He calculates and calculates, more precisely than if he were going to operate on a patient's leg. He intends to record even his affection for his only daughter in his cash book. Supposing I had two, or even three or four, brothers, they would all have died insane before ever entering the Jesuits.

PHANTOM LEGS

Sa-Mi had no desire to go on thinking about Sok-Hun or her father. She turned to the next page of her text, suddenly brushing it with her fingers as if a strand of Sok-Hun's or her father's scruffy hair might be adhering to it.

On the day after the ball, Vanina noticed that her father, who was the most carefree of men and who had never in his life ever bothered to lock a door, was very carefully locking the door of a little stairway that led to an apartment on the third floor of the palace. That apartment had windows on a terrace adorned with orange trees. Vanina set out to make visits in Rome. On her return, the coach entered through the courtyards to the rear, the main gate being blocked with preparations for an evening illumination. Vanina looked upward and was astonished to see that one of the windows of the apartment that her father had so carefully locked, was standing open. Having rid herself of her lady-in-waiting, she climbed to the attics of the palace and after some searching succeeded in finding a little barred window looking out onto the terrace adorned with orange trees. The open window that she had noted was only two steps away. Someone must be living in that room. But who? On the next day, Vanina managed to gain possession of the key of a small door opening on to the terrace adorned with orange trees.

Windows looking out onto a terrace adorned with orange trees.... Chancing to look up, an open window, someone must undoubtedly be living in that empty room. But who can be living there?

Sa-Mi suddenly felt hot tears scalding her eyes. The printed words on the page were rising and falling like waves, blurred by the tears: *des fenêtres sur une terrace garnie d'orangers.*

Sa-Mi read on, repeating several times the words "windows" "room" "someone" and *"mais par qui?"* Strictly speaking, this passage in which Vanina happened to notice that one of the windows on the terrace adorned with orange trees was open could not be considered a poetic scene at all. It was a section that could only be read with the mixture of suspense, anxiety and dread foreshadowing some crucial incident often found in detective stories, or if not that, at least it awakened a strong curiosity. Yet Sa-Mi's eyes were moist and her voice trembled as if she were reading a sad romance.

An empty room covered in dust: I clearly saw that the window of a room in which no one had been living was suddenly open. I have never seen a terrace adorned with orange trees, yet I feel sure that those were orange trees. My heart, yes, my heart was a *petite fenêtre grillée*, was one of those empty rooms you enter with a shrinking sense of desolation, a room devoid of human warmth. Yet now those windows were open toward the terrace with its orange trees...toward those things resembling orange trees golden in the sunlight. At some point a stranger had come in, opened the window, and was lying there. Undoubtedly this room was inhabited by someone. But who on earth could it be? *Mais par qui?*

Sa-Mi had been thinking of Chon Hyon-Su. She had been thinking of fateful symbolic incidents like the moment when Vanina looked up in astonishment at that open window. Sa-Mi adopted the attitude of a student obliged to study for an exam, as if she sensed someone watching her, clasping a dictionary in one hand and straining to read the phrases that followed.

Vanina parvint à se procurer la clef d'une petite porte qui ouvrait sur la terrasse garnie d'orangers.

"*La clef*...the key...and Vanina." Professor K was talking about keys. "The fact that Vanina managed to gain possession of the key can be explained in a number of ways. It can be taken as simply suggesting the possibility that Vanina can now enter the room with the open window. If we view it a little more deeply, a little more symbolically, it can mean that she has grasped the clue that will open the doors of love. Interesting, is it not? This talk of opening signifies the opening of the doors of love, that world of love that Vanina at present has absolutely no awareness of. Speaking in simple terms, the key that she gains possession of obviously means the key to her first experience of love. But you must be careful of the grammar in this phrase."

What I had to be careful of was not grammar. It was that word, key. How my heart used to beat as I stood in front of the storeroom in our family home down in the countryside, closed by a rusty padlock. I suppose it was because I was a child. I was curious about everything, in particular if something was locked, firmly locked with a padlock, be it a storeroom, a chest, or a cupboard, I was overwhelmed with a desire to see inside. Only I had nothing in the way of a key that might serve to open the padlock. Even now, when I think of it I am certain that the pattern engraved on the brass padlock firmly locking the storeroom represented the face of a demon.

Every time I glimpsed that padlock, I was filled with a dread quite equal to my curiosity. With its horns, its two projecting fangs, and its bulging eyes, that savage face bore an expression forbidding anyone to approach. I tried shaking the door. The dull clunk of the rings against the padlock was like the sound of a stone sinking into a deep pond. After I had pulled at the door several times, the ring to which the padlock was fastened would yield and a crack big enough for my little wrist would appear between the two panels of the door. A gap in the storeroom door.

I used to stand for hours on end peeping through that crack into the dark storeroom. It was dark inside the storeroom, but where a ray of light penetrated through the gap the partial form of strange objects dimly appeared. Things glimmered as if deep under sea in the depths of that darkness, like the red coral I had seen in my coloring books. I could make out one corner of a strange painting on a hanging scroll, and a lengthy string threaded with beads. Perhaps because everything in that space closed to me by the padlock seemed strange and mysterious, I came to think of the objects lying concealed in the darkness inside the storeroom as possessing a host of secrets, so that they were like things belonging to the world beyond, not proper for human possession. Ah, then Vanina Vanini, and everyone, should never open locked doors with their keys. That locked door, all locked doors, ought always to remain firmly closed.

I suppose it was a day for a family memorial rite. It was the first time I had ever seen anyone open that mysterious storeroom. Rattling her bundle of keys, grandmother undid the rusty padlock in a very down-to-earth manner. To grandmother with her keys, something like a demon's face glowering with a fearful expression did not seem to be a problem. As she threw open the storeroom door, my mysteries in the dark evaporated completely. Shabby tables for offerings, covered with cobwebs and dust, and some common-or-garden candlesticks.... What I had taken for coral was a broken vase, while the bright string of beads was in fact the string of an old felt hat like those worn by rural folk-music performers. There was nothing there at all. Only things like the droppings of the mice that skittered through there all night long. Rusty, crumbling, moldy things from long, long ago. Nothing but things of that kind, and the darkness. Keys destroy all sense of mystery. While they trouble the silence, banish darkness and everything like it, keys can only confirm the emptiness. As Professor K said, neither Vanina nor I should ever have obtained the key that opened the doors of love.

She stole cautiously toward the still open window. She was concealed by one of the shutters. There was a bed at the far end of the room, with some one in it. Her first reaction was to withdraw; but then she noticed a woman's dress thrown over a chair. Examining more attentively the person lying in the bed, she perceived that it was someone with fair hair, and seemingly very young. She no longer doubted: it was a woman. The dress thrown over the chair was stained with blood; there was likewise blood on the woman's shoes that lay on a table. The stranger stirred; Vanina realized that she was wounded. Her breast was covered with a large blood-stained cloth, held in place by nothing but ribbons. Surely no surgeon's hand had set it there.

Vanina soon noticed that each day at about four o'clock her father shut himself up in his apartments, then made his way to the stranger; he soon came down again, and took the coach to visit the countess Vitteleschi. As soon as he was gone, Vanina would climb up to the little terrace, from where she could observe the stranger. She felt her affections deeply moved in favor of this unfortunate young woman, and tried to guess what might have happened to her. The blood-stained dress thrown over a chair looked as if it had been slashed with a dagger. Vanina could even count the number of holes. One day she saw the stranger more clearly: her blue eyes were gazing heavenward, she seemed to be praying. Soon her lovely eyes were filled with tears; the young princess had to make a great effort not to go and speak to her. The next day, Vanina ventured to conceal herself on the little terrace before her father arrived. She saw don Asdrubale go into the stranger's room, carrying a basket of provisions. The prince looked anxious and said little. He spoke in a voice so low that, although the French window was open, Vanina was unable to hear his words. He left at once.

"That poor woman must have terrible enemies," Vanina thought to herself, "for my father not to dare confide in anyone, despite his carefree character, and be obliged to climb one hundred and twenty steps every day."

A blood-stained book, a blood-stained cloth, and blood-stained shoes. As soon as she heard the word "blood" Sa-Mi recalled vividly the face of Chon Hyon-Su as he lay on the bed in his sick-room. She had not visited the room in secret out of curiosity like Vanina. It was April 18, and she had been looking down from the upstairs balcony when one of the demonstrating students, covered in blood, was carried into the clinic that formed part of the house. She had simply gone down to the clinic at the sound of her father's call, as she frequently did when there was an emergency and there was not enough nursing staff. It was not a bullet wound. Judging from the blood flowing thickly from his head he had probably been beaten with a club or the butt of a rifle, or perhaps he had been trampled underfoot. The students who brought him claimed that a band of the thugs backing up the police had set about them with pitchforks and chains as if they were a pack of dogs. Sa-Mi was completely accustomed to the sight of blood. Whether it was the blood flowing from a human body or the mercurochrome poured out of a bottle, there was no difference; they were equally red. Bloodstained bandages and dressings had been part of daily life since her infancy. Yet now, for the first and only time, blood, human blood flowing from lacerated human flesh, took on a completely new meaning and struck to the depths of her heart.

"*Il y avait aussi du sang...*" Professor K's French accent was always somewhat overdone. Especially the nasal sound when he pronounced *sang* was full of an elasticity suggestive of the lightness of a ballerina's crimson shoes rather than the stickiness of blood.

"You note how the partitive article precedes the word for blood. It indicates a particular quantity, that is, it serves to denote the limited amount of blood spread over the shoes lying on the table. Of course, as you will learn on reading further, this unknown wounded woman is none other than the *carbonaro*, soon to become Vanina's lover, Missirilli, who had escaped from Sant'Angelo prison."

Professor K was busy wiping away the word blood without the least emotion, grammatically (a word he often employed) and chattily, just like father wiping away the clotted blood from his scalpel with a scrap of sterile gauze without the least emotion. Yet I felt that sensation for the very first time. The pain associated with blood, more, the pain accompanying the blood flowing from a particular individual...and while blood is always blood, the sight of the blood flowing from those lips was an intolerably sadder thing. People are probably able to kill insects, grasshoppers and such, without a qualm because their blood is not red. I wonder if we human beings would be able to feel for human life if people did not have red blood? Perhaps we would be able to kill people as easily as we kill grasshoppers.

One evening, as Vanina was cautiously bending her head toward the stranger's window, their eyes met and all was discovered. Vanina threw herself to her knees and exclaimed: "I love you; I am devoted to you."

The stranger beckoned to her.

"I owe you so many apologies," Vanina cried, "my stupid curiosity must seem so insulting to you! I swear to keep your secret and, if you demand it, will never come here again."

"Who would not be happy to see you?" the stranger replied. "Do you live in this palace?"

"Surely," Vanina responded, "yet I see that you do not know me: I am Vanina, don Asdrubale's daughter."

The stranger looked at her in amazement, blushed deeply, then continued: "I beg you to permit me to hope that you will come to visit me every day; at the same time, I would prefer it if the prince remained unaware of your visits."

Vanina's heart was beating madly; the stranger's manners seemed full of marks of distinction. (...) The unknown woman told her she had received a wound in the shoulder that had penetrated as far as the lung and was causing her much pain. She frequently found her mouth full of blood.

Hyon-Su had opened his eyes, lying on the bed. His eyes were inflamed and red, and something like tears shone in them. His gaze strayed over the room's gray walls. Staring at me as I sat at the corner table he spoke for the first time.

"Are you a nurse?"

"No, I'm the doctor's daughter."

"Then why are you all the time looking after me like this? You were here yesterday, and the day before as well."

"Please forgive me. Your eyes were always closed, I thought you were asleep. You mean that you've known I'm not a nurse for several days?"

Why did Hyon-Su feel obliged to view even me with eyes full of hatred? Perhaps because he had lost so much blood. People who lack blood view the world with an icy gaze, while those with too much blood view everything with a fiery glare. There has to be just the right amount of blood flowing through the veins.

"If it embarrasses you, I won't come again. I hope you won't misunderstand. Would it be all right to use the word friend? To see you as a friend of the same sex as myself, wearing a skirt and high heels, with her hair in a scarf?"

"Think as you please. Think of me as a boy, it's all right. Will you stay where you are? How shall I...."

Hyon-Su looked uncertain how to go on; he did not know what to call me. It was exactly the same expression as the stoic grimace of pain that he put on when they changed the dressings on his wounds.

It seemed to be an expression that had been habitual with him even before he was wounded.

"How shall I...what shall I call you?"

"Call me Sa-Mi, Choi Sa-Mi."

"Sa-Mi? It sounds like a stage name. The *Mi* must be the Chinese character for beauty, and is *Sa* the Sa for silk?"

"No, it's one of the characters for sand; not the one written with 'stone' as the radical, but the one that combines 'small' with the 'water' radical. I think it designates the fine sand at the water's edge."

"Sa for sand, sand at the water's edge, it's the first time I've come across that character. I asked your name and got that reply, well, I don't know if you'll like me saying it, but...well, really..."

"No, it's not because someone asked me about my name, I simply spoke first."

"Whichever it was, it doesn't matter. Let me just go on chattering to myself. It's quite all right for you to think of me as a girl and for me to think of you as one of those boys that I was in a mob with, shouting slogans together only a few days ago. And hey, you just called me 'someone.' Well, my name...."

"I know it already. I saw it on your medical record. And you're in your third year at S...University, that too. But you said, 'I don't know if you'll like me saying it...' What were you going to tell me?"

"Sand at the water's edge.... I was thinking of that Chinese character." Hyon-Su suddenly tried to raise himself in the bed, like someone startled by something. Seeing that the needle of his blood transfusion was about to pull out, Sa-Mi instinctively seized his shoulder and gently made him lie back on the pillow. It was as if a woman, no matter how young, was maternal by nature, even before she married and had children of her own. Sa-Mi herself was surprised by her professional skill as she seized the almost unknown boy's shoulder and without any sense of embarrassment helped him lie back on the pillow. Hyon-Su had shut his eyes. Is it on account of the blood? That blood flowing from his pale forehead? Is that why I feel so close to this stranger? No, it must rather be because of the gunfire. Because of the noise of pounding running feet. And also...

Spring flowers had been falling. Was it because they had been crushed by those muddy boots?

Hyon-Su spoke again, his eyes still shut.

"Sand at the water's edge, that was what you told me, wasn't it? I first saw the sea when I was five. Standing on the white sand at the water's edge, I saw the blue sea, the vast, deep blue sea off the southern coast. Then when I was ten, I saw barley fields. I was walking between barley fields, clasping my starving belly. There I was, ten years old, obliged to walk along that rural path pressing my empty stomach and longing to see the fields ablaze with gold, urging the barley shoots to grow quickly and ripen quickly. When we ran out of reserves of grain in early spring, even the rats used to leave our house for somewhere else. People used to say I had an odd way of thinking; I used to think about life with my empty guts. I was ten when I saw those green barley fields. Standing on a hillside of bare red clay studded with scrubby bushes, chewing a mouthful of pine needles, I saw those green fields of barley rocking just like the waves of the sea. It's all right. Stay sitting as you are. Let me just go on chattering. What I wanted to shout, out there in the crowd, may not really have been the great, impressive slogans people in such mobs tend to cry. Now I'm twenty, twenty years old, and there was nothing at all I could see. I could see nothing but something like the sky on a cloudy day. I haven't seen that many girls. I haven't seen the books in the library. Can't you keep coming to see me here every day? Your father won't like it, though."

Sa-Mi felt an urge to cry out. Not in a soft voice, though. She longed to roar like the people in a huge crowd, even meaningless things. The windows were always closed. The room was empty. If she shouted, she felt as if the window panes would fly in splinters and a cool breeze come wafting in. She had the impression she would see a terrace adorned with orange trees. That she would be able to see something like green plants alive with golden sunlight and beetles. The breath issuing from Sa-Mi's lips was warm like alcohol.

"I want to chatter away, too. Why, we're friends."

Hyon-Su opened his eyes and stared Sa-Mi in the face. But Sa-Mi was looking up at the black blood as it flowed down the tube into Hyon-Su's body. It might be blood, but how was it that the black bags of blood she took from the fridge or that they bought at the blood bank were that dreadful color? The blood they contained was like dead blood.

"What makes you think of me as your friend? Were you out demonstrating like us? I hate hearing girls calling boys their comrades."

"No!" Sa-Mi exclaimed. It was so loud that she held her breath for a moment and deliberately stayed sitting still.

"Why, every time you speak, you begin with 'No'!"

"No! That's not what..."

"You said 'No' again!"

For the first time, Hyon-Su was laughing. Yet even as he laughed, a hint of pain still lurked about his lips, like when they removed the dressings that had stuck to his wounds. Was it because traces of blood still remained on his lips?

"Not that. I want to talk about the blood."

"Did I loose a lot of blood? As a rule I'm very careful about my blood; selling blood is my occupation."

Gazing up at the black blood in the transfusion bottle, Hyon-Su spoke in tones of self-derision.

"I suppose that blood too belonged to someone who received a number at a hospital door, joined a queue, then waited and waited before finally exchanging it for a few banknotes. It may even be my own blood, the bottle that I sold to the blood bank a few days ago. Now I've bled a lot and not got a penny for it, when it should have been sold to a hospital. This blood staining my dressings too."

"That wasn't the kind of blood I meant. When you were lying in the emergency ward with your face all covered in blood, while father (he's Dr. Choi) and the nurses were busily mopping up the blood and trying to staunch the bleeding, I glimpsed what blood meant for the very first time. I didn't see the sea when I was five. I didn't see barley fields clutching my hungry stomach when I was ten. But now I'm eighteen, it's just a few days since I was eighteen, and aged eighteen I saw blood. That's all. So I came to think of Hyon-Su, who was lying there bleeding, as my friend. That swollen face? Once the swelling goes down, when your black eyes fade, after they remove the stitches from your wounds, like the face you had in times gone by: those are faces I do not know. Those faces are unknown to me. If I thought of you as a friend, it was because I realized that human blood needs no kind of expression. There is no reason why blood should have eyes, or a nose, or a mouth. After all, there are cases, it all depends, when we are more vividly struck, more deeply impressed by things without shape than by those with. Indifferent people normally find blood revolting. Although there are others, like my father, who don't even feel revolted by it. It's merely someone else's blood. But there are times when you see someone's blood flowing and experience pity. When you experience feelings toward another person that are human yet detached, you no longer feel their blood to be revolting, instead you feel pity."

"You mean that you saw my blood and felt pity? And so you felt comradeship, you wanted to call me your friend? Otherwise you would have found it revolting..."

Sa-Mi once again said, "No!"

"No. It was sorrow. And pain. That was the first time I had ever felt sorrow and pain at the sight of someone bleeding. I can't explain why it should have happened. Yet one thing is clear. When you see someone's blood with feelings of sorrow and pain, you cannot simply think of that person as just anybody. We had already become friends in that moment."

"What a genius Stendhal is! To pretend that a man of letters can have no skill in mathematics is a patent lie. Um, how shall I put it? Yes, we may say that a novel is a kind of linguistic mathematics or geometry."

Professor K spoke in tones of admiration, fingering the knot of his frivolously red tie with chalky fingers.

"Only think. Vanina is an aristocrat's daughter. Moreover, she is the kind of girl whose only thought is to make a fool of any man she sets eyes on. With her black hair, blazing eyes, Vanina knows very well how beautiful she is. To make a digression, many women are not arrogant for all their learning while there is not one who is beautiful without being stuck up. Beauty is a woman's main talent. What I am saying may seem to be insulting, but a girl who has only a minimum of education will tend to despise men even more than you university graduates, once she is sure of her looks. That as an aside; now let us examine for a moment Stendhal's precise calculations."

It was autumn. In the garden visible beyond the windows of the classroom, salvias were blooming. Those scarlet salvias were not so much autumn flowers, they were more like the leftovers of summer, the ashes remaining after summer had gone up in flames. Their every petal seemed to be saturated with memories of torrid summer days.

"First, at the point where the text says that one *carbonaro* has escaped from Sant'Angelo prison, it merely says that he had disguised himself. If it had been explicit from the beginning that he had disguised himself as a woman, Vanina would surely have guessed that he was the carbonaro on discovering Missirilli in her house wearing women's clothing. Second, it is a very fine calculation to have disguised Missirilli the escaped convict as a woman. Without that, how on earth could the proud Vanina ever have had a chance of coming in contact with the man, himself proud as we were saying previously? Taking him for a woman, Vanina feels safe and associates with him. As a result, the process by which Vanina falls in love with the *carbonaro* follows quite naturally, does it not? The escaped prisoner's disguising himself as a woman seems quite natural; as a consequence, the haughty Vanina's frequentation of his room from the very start feels equally natural. It's all a matter of double play. Third, Stendhal is thereby killing three birds with one stone. Vanina really takes Missirilli for a woman. Now an ugly man will never be taken for a woman, no matter how pretty the women's clothes he puts on. It is not just a matter of saying that he disguised himself as a woman; the disguise suited him so well it suggests automatically that he was sufficiently handsome for Vanina to fall for. Vanina was completely taken in by Missirilli dressed as a woman. The fact that she could be taken in like that is at the same time the guarantee that he was sufficiently good looking for her to fall in love with. Such admirable skill. Now, I must make a modification in what I said. Stendhal's novel is not linguistic mathematics; it's linguistic economics, economics. What skill, to dress a man in some women's clothing and make that serve such multiple functions. If you employ that degree of skill in your housekeeping after you are married, you will find yourselves able to wear diamond rings even larger than those worn by don Asdrubale with what you get from your husbands' meager pay packets."

Once again, Professor K looked as if he were waiting for his students to laugh. But Sa-Mi had not laughed. Gazing at the red salvias, she thought to herself how blood has the power to transform a man into a girl's closest friend without any need for him to dress up in women's clothing. That was how it must have been for Vanina. A blood-stained book, blood-stained shoes, a blood-stained cloth, a blood-stained cloth covering the breast: that was the reason why Vanina had found herself able to fall in love with that unknown woman, or rather that dangerous *carbonaro*.

At last Sa-Mi's eyes reached the passage where Missirilli reveals his true identity.

LEE OYOUNG

While she read the passage—it had been the same during the lecture—for some reason the soft and lusterless voice of Hyon-Su rang in her ears. His voice seemed to issue less from his throat than from the very bottom of his lungs. That voice emerged from the letters of her text. Perhaps because Hyon-Su too had kept repeating almost mechanically: "It would be unworthy of me to deceive you."

"Why, it would be unworthy of me to deceive you. I am called Pietro Missirilli, I am nineteen years old; (...) I'm a carbonaro. Our secret assembly was raided; I was brought in chains from Romagna to Rome. Thrown into a cell where a lamp burned day and night, I spent thirteen months there. One charitable soul had a mind to help me escape. They dressed me as a woman. Just as I left the prison and was passing the guards at the last gate, one of them cursed the carbonari. I slapped his face. I assure you it was no act of bravado but quite simply a thoughtless moment. Pursued by night through the streets of Rome, wounded by their bayonets, already weakening, I made my way up into a house where the door was open; I heard the soldiers coming in after me so I jumped down into a garden. I fell just a few steps away from a woman who was walking there. (...)

I feel very ill. These last few days the bayonet wound in my shoulder has been hindering my breathing. I am going to die and I am in despair since I shall no longer see you."

Vanina had listened impatiently, then rapidly left the room. Missirilli found no trace of pity in those eyes, lovely though they were, but only the expression of a haughty character that has just been offended.

With her chin posed on the French dictionary, Sa-Mi closed her eyes in order to retain Hyon-Su's voice; it had rung out in

134

her memory and was vanishing again. The voice was agitating her heart, like the sound of a window being rattled by the passing wind on a winter's evening. Like a doctor wielding alcohol-soaked cotton-wool swabs in his forceps, Hyon-Su wielded a variety of words, thrusting them down onto Sa-Mi's young heart. Her breast tingled.

"Why, you're a bit late today....If I go down one corridor and cross the garden, I'll find Sa-Mi's room. All day long, that's all I've been thinking, lying here. I've been waiting for you, because I wanted to express more of what I've got stored up inside. First, I wanted to tell you frankly that I don't like girls and things like that. Although I say it like that, I don't suppose you will feel it concerns you.... Did I tell you last time how I've reached a point now I'm twenty when I'm incapable of seeing anything.... But speaking bluntly, who ever heard of a twenty year old boy that didn't think of girls? There have been many times when I've spent the whole night thinking of girls. You told me that seeing me bleeding you experienced a deep sense of friendship, but I've come to realize that I'm someone who has absolutely no wish to receive even that kind of friendship from either girls or boys. I tell you, I'm someone who detests flowers because flowers are beautiful, and who detests snow because it's white and pure.

"Suppose we talk about flowers. Flowers blossom anywhere. It must have been about two weeks ago. I had been taken to the police station, on suspicion of organizing a demonstration at the university. I'll not tell you what happened there. If I started to tell you that, I'd have to describe in just how cowardly a way I behaved. Anyway, not being able to take much pain and contempt, I decided to sign an undertaking not to do such things again on a sheet of gray paper they gave me. I had no seal with me, so I was obliged to press my thumb on the red ink pad and sign the undertaking with that. Just as I was pressing my thumb on the paper underneath my name, what do you think I saw? Flowers blossoming out in the back yard of the police station. I could see springtime flowers out in that yard through gaps in the paper covering the windows....if you ask me their names, I'll tell you.... I saw red and yellow spring flowers blooming. My cheeks were swollen and red. My hands were shaking, I could scarcely move my legs, but the point is that those flowers blooming out there were quite indifferent to my sufferings. To see flowers like that in such a place is the last thing you would expect, surely. In a place where there's nothing but criminals and people busy dealing with criminals; a place full of tense nerves and grim shadows like an iron cage. There they were, those spring flowers blossoming, completely indifferent to the squeaking chairs and the dark corridors, the screams and the papers and everything else. When I first glimpsed those flowers with their serenity, I nearly burst into tears. Then I felt a kind of fury rising in my throat, a feeling of rejection, of resentment, of betrayal before those indifferent flowers. To think that flowers blossom everywhere and anywhere, quite indifferent to human sufferings, inconsistencies, hardships.... I even felt a sense of unfairness. To say something forms relationships with nothing is as much as to say it forms relationships with anything. The girls I met in my adolescence were just the same. Girls are pretty, they're as warm as your own home, and serenely fragrant too. There's no doubt about it. But they are quite unrelated to the tragedy of our history. It occurred to me that girls are a kind of paradoxical flower: capable of loving any and every one because they love no one. The more pretty girls I see, the more girls pretty as Sa-Mi I see, the more I feel disgruntled and overwhelmed with chagrin. Don't think I'm saying it's because girls aren't pure. It's because they are pure that girls get corrupted. I can't begin to tell you how much I used to love snow when I was a kid. I have an impression the snow-flakes I saw as a child were a lot bigger and softer and whiter than those I saw as a teenager. I could not help feeling regret when I saw how that snow got trodden by muddy boots and turned into a dirty slush. No, not just regret, it was a kind of rage. The snow was so clean and pure, which was unable to offer any resistance. Because it was so chaste it got trodden underfoot, melted in a flash, became soiled and turned into muddy sludge. Generally speaking, that's what happens to chaste women too.

"Today I'm going to have to limit myself to talking about the things I dislike. It would be unworthy of me to deceive you. The fact that I don't like doctors; that I don't like places like clinics and hospitals; not even this clinic where you live.... I have the feeling that I must tell you all these things. Sa-Mi, you must understand all that. Why are doctors' waiting rooms so empty? They're always empty, aren't they, no matter whether there are people in them or not? And the fuller they are of patients, the deeper and vaster their emptiness becomes. A few magazines and newspapers are laid out without fail on the table for people to read, but the patients don't touch them; they just sit there vacantly as if they were dazed, staring at the ceiling or the walls, waiting for hours on end. The sound of children crying, the sound of people coughing, trying to clear their throat of something.... Sa-Mi, you must have seen a lot of faces: the gaunt faces of undernourished patients, and the wretched faces of patients sitting anxiously waiting for their turn. While the doctors, or at least the one that I know, rake up a lot in that emptiness. Sick people, even adults, go back to being like children in the presence of a doctor. They make a fuss, they exaggerate their symptoms in hope of gaining sympathy, or they try to behave in a dignified way like children eager for praise. Yet doctors show no feelings, at least not the one I know. He used to exploit his patients' pain and innocence to the maximum extent. He seemed to have his stethoscopes in his ears not in order to heal diseases but to tame them.

"You'd best not listen to what I'm saying. A lot of times the so-called confessions are meant for oneself to hear, rather than for other people. You often have to listen to yourself. You said that you felt friendship on seeing me bleeding, but now you have to listen to what I say. You have to listen to my words, not my blood. Now maybe even that friendship will fade away too. Yet for some reason I feel that I want to strip away all my disguises in your presence.

"That clinic: the doctor that I know is someone who hired me as his children's private tutor as soon as I was accepted at S University. My mother died in poverty, and I should by rights have done the same. But I have the impression that I went to work in the family at that clinic because I had decided to cling to life for a long time in order to take my revenge on poverty. If that doctor had not been an unlicensed quack, or if the patients going there had not looked so shabby and sad, I might not have had this intense prejudice against hospitals, yours included. Here you're in Hyoja-dong, and this clinic's in a high class area, so you may not be able to understand what I'm talking about. That clinic was at the foot of a hillside covered by a slum. Prostitutes, day-laborers, people who had tried to kill themselves by swallowing poison, undernourished children, people suffering from ringworm and boils, whose wrists, when they rolled up their sleeves for an injection, were invariably marked by protruding purple veins. The chests touched by his stethoscope bore the dark shadow of the rib cage. No matter what patient came, that quack earned his money by giving them a jab of penicillin, making them take an aspirin, a digestive powder, and ground-up vitamin pills he bought at the pharmacy. And that's not the full reason why I have this hatred and prejudice against hospitals and doctors. Whenever some hometown friend paid a visit to the clinic to flatter that quack on his success, I invariably had to be displayed before the guests as a token of it. I still remember the order of events. When guests arrived at the clinic, first the quack would show them his two-story clinic, so spick and span it didn't fit in with the shacks in the slum though it was illegal, like them. After that he would call out, 'White!' White was the name of the household dog. He claimed that its pedigree was more precisely recorded than any human being's. That dog was a pure-bred French poodle. It would never eat anything but fat meat and caught a cold if it slept outdoors. Didn't he use to say that there were less than ten dogs like his in the whole of Seoul? And one of them belonged to him. That White was a sort of badge testifying to his success. He would tell how the dogs belonging to the speaker of the National Assembly and to the head of some big corporation, as well as those of a minister and of a certain ambassador, were all related to his White. And those visitors would cast envious looks at that quack as if he himself were directly related to the speaker of the National Assembly, or a minister, or the head of some corporation. But that was not what I found so wretched. That's not the reason why I spoke of hatred. I soon got used to all that. What I could not endure was knowing fully well that after White it would be my turn. I was going to have to stand on the very spot where the dog had been obediently squatting at his feet, its tail wagging and its tongue lolling out, witnessing to the quack's glory and success. When I heard the call 'White.... White!' from downstairs, I knew it would be my turn next. I would soon be obliged to get up from the study table where I was giving the children their lesson. Once the calls for White had died away, I would soon be hearing the call for 'Mister Chon.' Ah, 'Mister Chon.' Then for absolutely no reason I would be obliged to go and stand in front of the visitors and make my pointless bows like some kind of criminal. The quack doctor would introduce me: 'This is our children's private tutor. He is a freshman at S University and he was most specially recommended, most specially, by the dean, with his future prospects in mind, to be in charge of our children's education.' Then those poor visitors would open their eyes wide, just as they had nodded their heads in amazement, as if exclaiming in loud tones at the sight of White's thick, smart, oily fur; nodding their heads as if signing a certificate attesting to how greatly that quack doctor had succeeded.... Before I finally left that clinic and its family, I stroked White's head as a sign of farewell, thinking: who knows? If I had been unconscious of suffering, of insults, of shame like a dog, like a purebred poodle, perhaps at least I might have been able to live the same kind of elegant life, refusing to eat anything except fatty meat and catching a cold if I ever slept outside...and I could have become your lifelong friend. But when I ran away from that clinic, do you think I could really escape from those patients' faces, and White with his wagging tail, and the stares of those rural visitors with their lack of imagination who arrived with their exclamations prepared in advance? While I had left that place behind me, I soon came to realize that the whole world was just like that quack doctor's clinic, that healthy people were all like him while the sick were all like that clinic's patients. There was no escape. Yet I was quite unable to get rid of the idea that I ought to set up new hospitals in a new land. That's why I found myself obliged to go charging forward in the midst of all the tear-gas. I was obliged to shout until I was hoarse, running toward those clubs and heavy boots and horses' hoofs, until I shed that blood that you saw flowing. But Sa-Mi, I have to make a confession, just one: I was never in the least bit brave. No one brave would ever go chattering words idle as tears to some girl while all the time saying he hated it, lying rigid as a corpse with legs and arms in plaster like this. People like that have already left the world. They're the ones who died. It was unique because I would have felt ashamed in their sight that I couldn't run away. I was the one who stirred up the demonstration. Yet here I am, still alive and speaking, while all others are dead. And Sa-Mi, the worst of it is that I'm forced just to lie here, in the thing I hate most of all, a hospital, saying how grateful I am. Suppose I can't pay for my treatment? I never once saw any of those prostitutes or day-laborers come to that quack for treatment empty-handed. Even after the plaster is off and the stitches are removed from my cuts, I'll not be able to move about freely. I'm someone who ought to have died. In future you'd better not call me your friend."

Yet the expression in Hyon-Su's eyes showed not the slightest trace of wanting any sympathy. Proudly, as if in scorn, as if to say that he scorned even the daughter of this clinic's owner, he gazed at Sa-Mi. She rose, shuddering to think that he had been bleeding, that his face had been battered, long before she had ever seen him, long before he was carried into their clinic, long long before.

One evening, although by now Missirilli was much improved and Vanina no longer had the pretext of fearing for his life, she ventured to come alone. At the sight of her, Missirilli was filled with happiness, but he took care to hide his love; his prime intention was not to loose the dignity becoming of a man. Vanina, who had come in with a blushing countenance and fearing tenders of affection, was taken aback at the expressions of friendship, noble and devoted, it was true, but far from tender, with which he had received her. When she left, he made no effort to retain her. (...)

Far from being obliged to impose limitations on the young carbonaro's ardors, Vanina found herself wondering if she loved alone (...), but was quite unable to take upon herself the decision to stop seeing him.

Even after that, even after hearing those words, which could be considered insulting to her if taken as such, whether it be his dislike of girls or his dislike of hospitals, Sa-Mi continued to frequent Hyon-Su's sick-room whenever the nurses were absent. Indeed, that explains why her original friendship was rapidly turning into feelings of love. When he was asleep, she would sit at his bedside knitting, examining his face from which the bruises were slowly fading. She felt that underneath the sticking-plasters he had a very open forehead. His eyebrows were thick and black, while his brow bore a slightly melancholy frown that made his nose look considerably higher than it was. His lips were still swollen. Remarkably small lips, they seemed likely to suit him if he ever disguised himself as a woman like Missirilli. He had no need of any further treatment. Her father had a good head for business. Journalists had come, contributions had been made, April's revolution was already over, so there was no sign of interest from the government or the police. The longer such a patient stayed confined in the hospital, the bigger the figures in the account books. If it would make the figures bigger, Sa-Mi's father was the kind of man who would have been quite content to have even his daughter as a patient. At least, Sa-Mi thought so.

"Ah well!" she finally told herself, "If I see him, it's for myself, for my own pleasure; I will never confess to him all the attraction he inspires within me." She duly paid long visits to Missirilli, who addressed her in the same way he might have done with twenty other people present. One

evening, after having spent the whole day detesting him and swearing to herself to be colder and severer with him than normal, she told him that she loved him. Soon she had nothing left to refuse him.

"Will you read me a book?"

When Hyon-Su said that, I would deliberately choose a book on philosophy or sociology, something having nothing to do with love, to read to him. But he pretended not to notice. If he had been like Sok-Hun, he would probably have asked me to read *Eveline* or *Annabel Lee* or, worse still, *Lady Chatterley's Lover*. I would have hated it if he had asked for books like that, but the indifference with which he pretended not to notice my perversity in reading him books dry as dust about nineteenth century conceptual philosophy was loathsome in the extreme.

When he felt like talking, he would go rattling on for hours on end, with no concern for what I might be feeling and then, while I was adjusting the flowers at his bedside or straightening his sheets, he would shut his eyes without a word of thanks and fall asleep. It was the last evening of April. My father had gone on a distant home call, and the nurse was outside washing bedspreads, while the two of us were gazing through the sickroom window. The April night air felt soft and slippery, like the foam rising from washing soap. Hyon-Su's arms and legs had been freed from their plaster, and I was holding his wrists, helping him to practice walking as if he were a little child just learning to toddle. His hands were cold. That only made me more aware of the feverish heat of my own scorching palms.

"Open your hands. Move your arms."

An old-fashioned tram was passing merrily, bluish sparks flying from its arm into the darkness.

"There's nothing wrong with me now. Just look."

Hyon-Su was gradually raising his arms, freed at last of their burden of plaster, toward my shoulders. At each movement, I felt his muscles grow tense with compact energy then relax, until I sensed their full power bearing down on my shoulders. Then his lips, I felt the touch of his lips like flowing blood.... I had closed my eyes and was recalling how his face had looked with blood flowing from between his lips. I was recalling my very first glimpse of that face, as he lay prostrate on the bed in that same sickroom. This physical body of ours, what is there about it that makes it capable of stirring up a person's feelings as it does, stirring them up like a mush of stewed beans? Hyon-Su had spoken of seeing the sea off the south coast when he was six, the sunlight breaking on its blue waves, and the sea breathing the wind away into the endless distance. Now, like some ship slowly sinking below that sea, I was rolling and foundering body and soul. I was wrapped in undulating fronds of green seaweed. Hyon-Su's hands and breast and lips and all had wrapped themselves about me like seaweed, like some mysterious kind of seaweed that no one can ever escape from once they are caught. It was just the same sweetish taste as kelp. It was an ocean, a world, a beach of white sand that I had never trodden before.

"Sa-Mi, is this possible?"

"I don't know. This is the warm sea that you saw in the south such a long, long time ago when you were only six years old. The wind is blowing. My hair is floating in the breeze."

Missirilli no longer had any thought of the duty he owed to his manly dignity. He loved as one loves for the very first time at nineteen and in Italy. (...) One day, Missirilli began to wonder: "What am I going to do? Stay hidden in this way in the home of one of the most lovely beings in Rome? Then the foul tyrants who kept me for thirteen months in a prison without once letting me see daylight will think that they have discouraged me! Woe to you, Italy, if your sons abandon you for so little!"

The revolution was over and people looked just a little happier than before. Sa-Mi realized very well that it was not simply on account of the fresh young leaves of May. The schools had opened again, too. On examination, absolutely nothing had really changed. Indeed, in some respects things had grown even more confused than before. Yet just as life is preparing for springtime inside a bulb that seems outwardly as hard as stone, it was evident that some unforeseeable change was burgeoning within people. On her way home from school, Sa-Mi saw students standing in the streets collecting donations.

For the victims of the events of April 19, those who had survived seemed to be ready to make almost any reparation in an attempt to draw a veil over their guilt-stricken hearts. Sa-Mi too, though she felt slightly ridiculous, opened her purse, drew out whatever banknotes her hand happened to grasp, and thrust them into the collection box. Covered with white paper, the square collection boxes looked exactly like the caskets that had contained the ashes of the dead.

"How can doing that ever make up for their lost youth? How could I think I'm going to make even one thousandth part, one ten-thousandth part of their destiny mine with these few banknotes?" The thought struck her that she had to go home, home to where Hyon-Su was waiting for her. As she stood there wavering, she was suddenly shocked to feel a hand touch her breast: a filthy, muddy hand. It was a beggar. Beggars always loom up from nowhere. The beggar, his face a mass of boils, seemed to be a kind of mute. He was waving his hand at Sa-Mi and roaring like an animal. He was probably asking for money. She found some change and was about to offer him a few small coins, when the beggar thrust her hand aside and pushed past her. Only then did Sa-Mi understand why he had been acting in that fashion. She was standing in front of the box for donations, blocking his access, and he was telling her to get out of the way. The beggar stood trembling for a moment in front of the box, then fumbled at the waist-band of his tattered trousers as if trying to catch lice. Crumpled banknotes emerged. It must have been his whole day's take from his begging. The beggar set about forcing the hand clasping the money down into the wooden casket of a collecting box that recalled a kind of piggy bank. Astonished, Sa-Mi was on the brink of exclaiming out loud. That this beggar, who had spent his whole lifetime begging from people, should contribute even one penny to help others, was a pure miracle. That wretched beggar, who normally lay prostrate at the roadside, grasping at one person's ankles after another, entirely dependant on the alms they deigned to spit at him, was giving away his money for people who had never seen his face, who had not the slightest idea of his name or where he came from. What power possessed him? Here was a man who had only ever received, giving like that.

"Hyon-Su, I nearly wept. While that poor beggar was stuffing his precious money into the collection box, all he had got by begging and being spat at in return, his mournful eyes were turned aside so as not to see the money, not to see that money passing through the slot in the collection box. And suddenly his eyes met mine. I nearly wept, really I did. It was so amazing, so pitiful. I feel like calling it the April Miracle."

Hyon-Su leaped roughly forward as if intent on taking me in his arms, and cried out.

"Sa-Mi! I've just realized: I'm young, we're young! Until now I've lived completely unaware of being young, I never once thought about it. Now, it's May.... If only this month of

May could last a whole lifetime. Is it really not possible for these budding leaves not to open any further, for the green of the grass not to get any darker, for the air to go on forever vibrating like this? How old did you say you were?"

"Eighteen! Why, there's that popular song: 'In her eighteen year old breast, the flowers are in bloom.' Whenever I used to think of it, I thought it was so silly it gave me the creeps. I used to laugh at it. But now I come to think about it, there's nothing funny about it after all, is there? What other words could I possibly use to express the things I'm feeling at present?"

"And I'm twenty, I'm twenty. That's not just my official age, either...."

Hyon-Su crushed me in his arms as he repeated, "Twenty, twenty!" over and over again. For the first time in my life I paid no heed to the sound of slippered steps in the corridor, or to my father's cough, not even to the stare of the nurse when with weasel-like stealth she opened the sick-room window and without any warning stuck her head in. Even if we had been standing out in the middle of the road, we would have embraced in the same way, unrestrainedly, regardless of who was looking.

"Let's go for a walk. I'm really perfectly all right now. I ought to have left already. If I'm still confined to this sick-room, it's because I need to be treated for another wound, the one I got because of you. Of course, it's going to take much longer to heal than any outside wound. As for the plaster—if you break an arm or a leg, you only have to put a cast on the broken limb and that's enough, but I was thinking how people wounded by love need to be put in plaster from head to foot. Yet...but what was I going to say? That's right, I didn't mean to go on like that about plaster, I was saying that I wanted to go out. To see those streets again. I must walk again down those streets where my friends fell and where I shed my blood. The barricades have been cleared away, and this youth with his twenty years, this youth just beginning to learn about love, wants to walk along those wide pavements. But no running. We must tread cautiously on the land of new days to come, one step at a time, as if we were walking over fields where the grass was just beginning to grow. Otherwise God might feel jealous. The mounted troops, the clubs, the tear gas, the emergency decrees and all those things have been overcome. The long dark night of youth and love is over, and at least we have the right to experience this new morning."

"I was like a phantom until now. It's as if a woman could only start to find out who she really is when she falls in love with a man. Because it's only now that I start to feel I have a physical body. Out we go, the two of us together, anywhere. There is no one following us, no one listening to our conversations, no matter where we go. Out we go, now, quickly. I'm praying that this Maytime breeze will stay beside us forever. As for the past, that can be spat out like chewing gum after you've finished chewing it."

"If you spit out gum carelessly, it'll most likely stick to someone's clothing; so let's bury it for good. First bury it deep underground, like dead bones, then let's go out...."

It was very quiet among the trees. I suddenly glimpsed a little squirrel. They always look like toy animals. Hyon-Su was lying with his head on my knees, gazing up at the May sky as it flickered between the leaves. We stayed there like that in complete silence for a good hour. Even now I can still vividly feel the weight of his body hard against mine. I was murmuring to myself as I gently stroked the fresh scars on his brow. "My goodness! Is it possible to love even a scar, then? Which part of this man do I love? Is it these scars? Or is it the unscarred skin, so perfectly smooth, not like a man's at all?" I watched the squirrel climb a tree trunk and thought the sun would never set in that Maytime woodland.

Vanina had no doubt that Pietro's greatest happiness must be to remain forever attached to her; he seemed far too happy.

It must already be after midnight. Sleep was weighing on her eyes. But as soon as her eyes encountered the passage where Missirilli prepares to leave Vanina, she felt herself grow tense again. Her eyes began to glisten as she peered at the French text. Besides, Professor K had been suffering from a bad cold when he had taught that portion of the text and there were many phrases she had not been able to grasp. As a result, she had to keep referring to the dictionary and every time she opened the dictionary, she would drop into memories of Hyon-Su.

"In this conversation with Missirilli, there is the phrase *dès que la nuit sera venue* which needs to be explained grammatically; *sera venu(e)* is the future perfect tense of the verb *venir* while *sera* alone is *le futur simple* the simple future tense of the verb *être*...so as you have learned previously, the future perfect signifies something that must happen before some other future event. As a result, you need to remember that normally the future perfect is used in contrast to a simple future tense. Koreans have no concept of such tenses, and that constitutes a large handicap in learning French. For us, past, present, and future are all ambiguous and vague. Especially the future, it seems.... Just to see the Korean grammar, and you get the impression that our people have always lived without any awareness of time or future. We have native Korean words to designate 'yesterday' and 'today,' but the word for 'tomorrow' comes from the Chinese, doesn't it? That alone seems to be closely connected to the fact that we have few ways of expressing the future."

As I listened to Professor K's grammatical explanations, I remember saying inwardly to myself, "Yes, what you say is surely right. We Koreans definitely seem to live without any awareness of the future. Sudden as autumn showers, suddenly the future changes. With no simple future, and no future perfect, in one way or another the future is always a dreadful mess."

Missirilli looked rather embarrassed as he addressed Vanina.

"As soon as night falls, I must go out."

"Take care to return to the palace before daybreak; I will be waiting for you."

"By daybreak I'll be several miles from Rome."

"Very good," said Vanina coldly, "and where do you intend to go?"

"To Romagna, to take my revenge."

"Since I am rich," she continued, perfectly calmly, "I hope that you will accept weapons and money from me."

Missirilli looked at her for a few moments without blinking; then he threw himself into her arms, exclaiming, "Life of my life, you make me forget everything, even my duty. But the nobler your heart, the more fully you must understand me."

Vanina wept bitterly and it was agreed that he would only leave Rome on the following day.

"Hyon-Su left like that, too. Left suddenly, like the future perfect. Professor, do you know how it happened? It had been cloudy since early morning. I was setting off to go to school, about to pass the main gate when there was Hyon-Su waiting for me in the corridor outside his room. To tell me he was leaving the hospital! Or more precisely, he was leaving me. Immediately, too. Of course, you know about the future tense, so you know that it's impossible for a patient to stay in hospital one or two months after making a full recovery. A hospital is not a hotel. I knew that. It's a matter of the simple future. That was not what made me sad. It was the way he replied when I asked why he was suddenly leaving. He had decided to leave today a long time before; he was simply telling me now. He had all the time been there at my side, talking, walking, reading together; but he had drawn a mental circle round today's date in his calendar all on his own. That was what made me so sad. Can you imagine what I felt? What it's like to be someone who does not know about the future? Can you imagine what I felt, when I found myself confronting that moment as it came barging in so abruptly, slapping me in the face, barging in without the slightest warning, so that I couldn't decide if it was future or present? So of course I said what I did. Let's wait a few more days. If you leave here immediately, you have no boarding-house room, no rent money, nothing for your food and clothing, do you? Until now we've only thought of each present day, haven't we? We've never once sat down together and thought about tomorrow, have we? At that, Hyon-Su admitted that he had been intending to leave secretly...that he should have left secretly, so that my face did not get in the way of the tasks he had ahead of him. Yet still he insisted that he loved me. At that I echoed that *dès que la nuit sera venue*, murmuring that we should talk that evening, and rushed out into the street.

"So please, Professor K, grammatically speaking, what form of the future tense corresponds to Hyon-Su's and my future? Can I ask you that?"

Sa-Mi found the passage where Vanina asks Missirilli to marry her.

"You certainly have a noble heart; all you lack is a correspondingly high position; I have come to offer you my hand and an income of two hundred thousand pounds. I will undertake to gain my father's consent."

Pietro threw himself down at her feet; Vanina was radiant with joy.

"I love you passionately," he said, "but I am a poor servant of my country; the more my country is unhappy, the more important it is for me to remain faithful to it. In order to obtain don Asdrubale's consent, think what a sorry role I would be obliged to play for years to come. Vanina, I must refuse you."

Missirilli hastened to commit himself. His courage was on the point of failing him.

"My great misfortune," he cried, "is that I love you more than life itself, that to leave Rome is the cruelest of all tortures. Ah! If only Italy were delivered from the barbarians! How gladly I would set out with you across the seas to go and live in America."

Vanina was paralyzed. His rejection of her hand had shocked her pride; yet a moment later she threw herself into Missirilli's arms.

Their next meeting was in a tea room, a gloomy place with no frills, in an outlying suburb. The air struck chill although it was May and other customers were sitting by themselves, waiting for people. It seemed that every one there was lonely. Sa-Mi's face grew red at the thought of what had happened there. What had made her speak so bluntly?

"Why did I suggest marriage so shamelessly? It still makes me blush just to think of it."

"We can get married. For years mother has lived in disgrace, treated as if she were almost not there. I am sure she'll stand up for me just this once. She's never had the right to lift her voice, all the time washing and washing the clinic's bloodstained sheets until she's grown old. It's all because she only had one girl, and no boy to inherit the hospital. But I'm sure she'll stand up for me this time."

"Don't you think we're still too young for that?"

"Now we're young, of course. But think how long it's going to take before we've got a new house built; we'll be older by then."

"A house."

"That's right, it'll be our house. With a garden where it'll always be May. And a bedroom where we can talk on and on in the evenings, on and on with no one to interrupt us. Where no one will be allowed to open the front gate without our permission."

"Ah, like in a monastery? A monastery where you only have to say your prayers and tomorrow comes tripping along?"

"Listen and don't laugh. You sleep late in the mornings, don't you? I've had to warm the coffee several times already. Here you are at last; you've not even washed your face, saying, 'Sugar, please, only one spoon,' like a child. You're such a lazybones; the only solution is for me to give you your breakfast in bed. Through the open window sunlight is shining softly, and a bracing morning breeze to wake you up...what music do you want? We sense that we're alive, that we're in love, that our warm bodies have not started to fade. We clearly see time and music whirling round us, always remaining in one place."

"Where's my study, then?"

The gramophone was not of the highest quality; music vaguely resembling Mendelssohn's Italian Symphony was emerging sweetly from it. The café was now completely empty and the woman in charge was adding up the day's takings under a feeble lamp.

"Where's my study, then?"

Hyon-Su seemed really curious.

"Upstairs. If you open the windows you can see the river....
You have this terrible habit of leaving your books lying about.
So I always have a hard time tidying up your study. Then you
look at the neatly arranged books and for some reason get
angry. 'You've put the books in any old order. I can't find where
any particular book is put. It takes me longer to find a book
than it does to read it.' Instead of thanking me, you complain."

Hyon-Su laughed.

"That's how it is. You women, so long as things look neat
and tidy, you think that's all that's needed. But you don't realize
that the books are arranged in complete disorder. You don't
realize that there's order in seeming disorder. It's because men
see the world in terms of concepts, while women see everything
in terms of emotion. It's funny. All that you're talking about is
what people call life."

"Our babies are too playful for words. If there's any noise
at all in the house, it's only the sound of the babies crying."

"Ah, family, wife, children, home."

As he spoke the words, Hyon-Su suddenly assumed a
strange expression composed of a mixture of melancholy and
hope. That expression was just like weather when the sun is
half covered with clouds.

"When I was small, I used to think that I wanted to live in a
western-style house, with a red-tiled roof in Dutch fashion. In
the village where I lived, there was a picture of a house like
that hanging framed in the barber's shop. In front of the house
there was a lake and on the lake a white yacht was gliding
along. But you know what I used to think? That there couldn't
really be a house like that anywhere in the world. That it was
nothing more than a fantasy painted by people as they dreamed,
like baby angels sprouting wings, or the bodhisattva Kuan-yin

standing on a cloud, or a flying carpet in the sky. There couldn't be houses like that, not anywhere in the world, because the only houses I knew were thatched huts stinking of fermenting soy malt. And when the summer rains came, centipedes would crawl into the rooms."

"Well, it's bad to be stubborn like that. Come on, shake off those kinds of prejudice and let's be going home. Father will be angry. He'll be upset simply because you're not a doctor, but we've already built our house. And father's too old to knock it down."

"Did Hyon-Su really turn down my suggestion of marriage with a heart like Missirilli's and leave me?" Sa-Mi wondered. It was already a long time ago, everything had faded and grown dim like the photos in an old album. There was surely a great difference between what had happened then, and the memories of their conversations or of his gestures that came to her as she read *Vanina Vanini* now. What ever must he have been thinking?

"What is one's country?" he wondered, "it's not like someone to whom we owe a debt of gratitude for some act of kindness, who might be unhappy and curse us if we fail to repay it. One's country and liberty, they're like my overcoat, something useful that I have to buy, true, if I have not inherited one from my father; in the end, I love my country and freedom because they are useful to me. If I don't need them, if they're like an overcoat in August, what's the point of buying them, and at such a high price? Vanina is so beautiful! She has such a singular genius! People will try to please her; she'll soon forget me. What woman ever had only one lover? These Roman princes that I despise as citizens have so many advantages over me! They must be

very pleasant company! Ah! If I leave, she'll forget me, I'll have lost her forever."

In the deep night, Vanina came to see him; he told her of the uncertainty he suddenly found himself plunged in, and the discussion to which, since he loved her, he had submitted the great word "country." Vanina was delighted.

"If he had to choose absolutely between his country and me," she thought, "I would win."

The clock of the nearby church struck three; it was time for their last farewells. Pietro tore himself from her. He was already on his way down the narrow stairs, when Vanina, holding back her tears, asked him with a smile:

"If you had been cared for by some poor country woman, would you do nothing to show your gratitude? Would you not try to repay her? The future is unsure, you are going out among your enemies: so give me three days in gratitude, as if I were a poor woman, to repay me for my pains."

"Let's stop talking of all that. I don't reckon I'll ever be someone happy to live like other men, someone with a family, raising children, let alone be the son-in-law destined to inherit a clinic and continue the name of the Choi Ho-Un Surgery. I'm someone who's chosen unhappiness. There has to be a new clinic built in a new land, with a new name for our sick babies with their masses of boils and their twisted limbs. For that, I've chosen hard, sad, lonely unhappiness. Maybe if I'd never seen that quack doctor, if I hadn't seen the sea when I was five, if I hadn't seen that barley field at ten, if I hadn't seen those spring flowers through the window of the interrogation room in the police station, then I could have spent long evenings talking with you about happiness. I could have slipped a ring on your finger and we could have gone strolling in the palace parks on

Sundays holding our kids by the hand and unwrapping caramels like ordinary people do. If ever days of health come when everyone's been treated for the diseases of history and been discharged healed, then I might hope to live like the colored silk threads in your sewing-box, those threads that contain a dream slowly becoming the pretty picture in an embroidery."

It was impossible to say whether either she or Hyon-Su had ever spoken such words. She rather suspected that the entire exchange was nothing but a fantasy, something that she had just concocted on the spur of the moment in a day-dream. What is certain is that he rejected her proposal of marriage, and that for almost a month after parting they heard nothing from one another, yet she remained firmly convinced that one day, sooner or later, Hyon-Su would live with her in his Dutch house.

Missirilli arrived at his destination still very sad; there he learned that the leader of the band had been arrested, and that he, a young man still scarcely twenty-eight years old, was about to be elected the leader of a band that included men of over fifty who had been involved in conspiracies ever since Murat's expedition in 1815. On receiving this unlooked-for honor, Pietro felt his heart begin to beat strongly. Once he was alone, he resolved never again to think of the young Roman woman, who had forgotten him, and to devote all his thoughts to his duty to "deliver Italy from the barbarians."

What makes men act as they do? They are determined to strut about not just with a tie round their necks, but with power too. In primary school they want to be head boy of the class. Once they enter middle school, they want to become sports stars and be applauded by everyone. There's no imagining how disappointed I felt on discovering that Hyon-Su was just another man like that. No, it was not disappointment. I felt sad. It must have been August. It was during the holidays. I was preparing to go off to the seaside. I urgently needed sunshine and ozone. My health was in a desperate state. Father had no need of patients of my kind. All he could deal with were patients with visible wounds.... I clearly recall it: I had gone to buy a swimming costume. There were broad brimmed straw hats, trailing blue and red ribbons. And beach robes striped in zebra patterns, as well as plastic beach-buoys in primary colors, inflated like balloons. And bikinis stretched over the breasts of mannequins. How brightly all those things shone in my heart! With luck, I'd be able to find pretty shells and perhaps, burying myself in the hot sand under a beach-umbrella. I would be fortunate enough to find that the sun, with its razor-sharp rays, made me forget everything. Then Hyon-Su came and shattered that illusion too. How could I have expected to meet him in that big store? There was Hyon-Su, waving casually as if we had met the day before; his gestures had become so elegant...waving and calling, "Sa-Mi." True, I had heard somewhere that the wounds he had received during the events in April had won him a high position in some student organization; but to hear him speaking the names of politicians as if they were his friends, putting on airs while affecting nothing of the sort, explaining that he had come here shopping because he was going to the beach, I found myself thinking that the boy aged ten who had seen a barley field clasping a hungry stomach had vanished from his life forever.

"I'm off to the seaside for a week or so; won't you come along with me? Of course, we're going in a group; there'll be six of us. You must know M; he's the party's public relations man. There's a lot of fuss about him in the papers every day, but he's not such a bad kind of fellow, really. And there'll be the head of the youth section too, but all the rest are student representatives, you'll get on all right with them. Nothing to feel embarrassed about. We'll just say we're engaged."

I hated the way the word 'engaged' emerged quite unashamedly from his lips, yet I had no choice but to accompany him to a restaurant as he suggested. As soon as they saw Hyon-Su, the white-coated waiters began to bow and scrape. He was obviously a regular customer. His present healthy face bore absolutely no resemblance to the bruised and swollen face with bloody lips I had seen in the hospital sick-room. I tried not to cry, but I felt something warm sliding down my cheeks. "I cannot hate this person. I cannot hate this person. So long as the wounds remain on his brow, so long as his bruised face remains in some corner of the sick-room, so long as the sound of him learning to walk again like a baby, walking up and down the corridor banging his crutches on the floor, continues to echo in some corner of a darkened room, I cannot hate this person." Hyon-Su's face had lost its previous appearance. It suddenly looked far sadder than before. What can this person be seeing now? Is he really discovering a new land and founding a new hospital on it? Is he going to hang up a sign indicating "The Chon Hyon-Su Surgery"? Won't there be a pedigree French poodle called White in that hospital?

"Hyon-Su, don't waste your youth. And don't think what I'm saying is pretentious. If ever you find yourself wounded again, don't fail to come back to the Choi Ho-Un Surgery, to that same sick-room. I'll be washing the sheets so that your bed is clean. Until my hands are swollen, until the skin peels, I'll wash those sheets for your bed until they're whiter than white."

"What do you mean, wounded? Why should I get wounded? Are you wishing me bad luck? It's because you bear me a grudge! I feel just the same. Why didn't you come to visit me? Is the future son-in-law always obliged to come and visit his future wife's house? I've taken the tram for Hyoja-dong many times. There was one evening; it was raining. The July rains seemed to be never going to end and the humidity in the air was making my old wounds ache. Late one evening I boarded the tram for Hyoja-dong, without even taking an umbrella. Squeezed between people like a sodden hound, shivering on account of the rain that had soaked me to the skin. Yet I had the impression that if I only met you I would feel warm. I was thinking of May, and how May would still be there in your garden. Only I didn't get out. By the time we reached the terminus, the only people left with me in the tram were an old woman in rags and some girls who looked like students from an evening school. I wiped the window with my palm and stared out into the dark, pressing my face against the glass with raindrops running down it. For a brief moment I saw the letters in the green neon sign "Choi Ho-Un Surgery" and your upstairs window with the light on go sliding past in the pouring rain. It was only visibly raining where the tram's headlight beams shone out. The raindrops sparkled as they fell like flakes of snow. But I didn't get out of the tram. If I meet you, if I'd met you then, I'd have been done for."

As I listened to Hyon-Su I clenched my teeth in an effort to control my tears. I was cursing myself for destroying my love by my pride. Trying to hide my feelings, I busily hacked at my steak and tried to get the resulting lumps of meat down my aching throat. As I did so, I experienced what salty tears are like. They taste better than meat; tears are much tastier. I deliberately tried to think humorous thoughts. I tried to cheer myself up, and as a result the tears soaked uncontrollably into the tablecloth! Hyon-Su! I longed for that day to be the last. After all, I was only eighteen.

She hastened to the home of one of her former chamber-maids, who had left her service to get married and open a small shop in Forli. Once there, she hurriedly wrote in the margin of a book of hours that she found in her room, the precise indication of the place where the band of carbonari was to meet that very night. She concluded her denunciation with the following words: "This band is composed of nineteen members; here are their names and addresses." After having written out the list, very accurate except that the name of Missirilli was missing from it, she said to the woman, of whom she was sure:

"Take this book to the cardinal-legate; he is to read what is written here and then return the book to you. Here are ten sequins. If ever the legate should pronounce your name, your death is certain. But if you enable the legate to read the page I have just written, you save my life."

Everything went perfectly.

I foolishly thought that I simply had to save him like Vanina. History was something that utterly falsified everything, like waves moving across the surface of the sea. Hyon-Su must surely realize that, but I longed to make him feel it directly. When they left for the coast, I stupidly went along with Hyon-Su's group. I was longing to provoke Hyon-Su. Looking back now, I can see more clearly what was in my mind at that time. It was blowing a gale. The sand came battering at the door of the villa all night long. Listening to the howling storm, I grasped Hyon-Su's hand and begged him not to get involved in politics and such. Tomorrow morning, go and look at the sea. Go and look at what has become of the foam on the waves, no matter how fierce and strong it is now. History was nothing more than a storm like this, which briefly shook the surface of the sea then vanished without trace. We needed to go down into the depths. I begged him: let's vanish forever in the ravines below the sea. They're calm and dark, but they're very precisely real. I suppose he didn't care for what I was saying. He abruptly called his companions into his room, claiming that he hated storms.

"When all's said and done, it's the way people feel that's the problem. Trying to have a serious conversation with these people who go about in overcoats in midsummer is just like telling a statue of Buddha in a temple to go and weed the fields."

The speaker was K, spiteful and shortsighted, who looked as though he had several pairs of eyes on account of the lenses of his glasses. He spoke angrily but in eloquently turned phrases. Surprisingly, Hyon-Su chimed in.

"After all, it would be all right if they were just ordinary overcoats. The main problem is that they're old-fashioned overcoats, like the one Napoleon wore when he set off for Moscow. It would be all right for people to wear overcoats even in summer, so long as they were modern-style ones."

"Still, at the moment we're being duped. Why are we all the time splitting up? What we have to be afraid of is not overcoats in summer or swimming costumes in winter; it's older people's beards. For a beard, summer and winter are all alike. Their lips are smothered in their beards; there's no knowing their true character. Anyway, we're still just learners. There's no call for us to go thinking about the problems of real politics for the moment."

Hearing the words of that flat-faced student spoken in a strong rural accent, I took courage and butted in. The outcome turned out to be unfortunate but at that moment I felt I simply had to speak up.

"It's not my place to speak, I know, but we can see that the students really are restless. An impatient gardener rubs off the buds while pruning the branches. We have to realize that the person who stays silent when all the others are in uproar is the one who shouts with the loudest voice. When the April Revolution was over, I saw people running through the streets dragging along with ropes the statue of a politician that they had knocked off its pedestal in a park. I reflected that it would be wrong if people went on and on dragging fallen statues through the streets. I'm convinced that the people who erected the statues and the people who pulled them down and dragged them around are all the same. The April Revolution as I conceive of it was not like that. The Revolution was the work of people knowing nothing of politics. That's why it was so pure. It was a Revolution without people dreaming of taking power. Now the students don't know what to do with their purity so they go selling it for next to nothing. I think what he says is right. When the heat of the earth is buried deep underground, it functions well, but when it comes breaking through to the surface it becomes a terrible volcano burning up people and forests and crops. Youth is not just a matter of being out on the streets; it's in the libraries, and on beaches like this, in rural woodlands and on river banks. Like he just said, I reckon that it's better not to get too close to real politics. I believe I have the right to speak like this as one individual student."

Outside the sandstorm was still blowing against the villa's wooden door. To hear the sound of the stormy sea, it seemed that the world was ending. Hyon-Su bounded to his feet.

"Look, here's another one wearing an overcoat. We're not stone Buddhas waiting to be dug up a thousand years later. Our bodies rot easily; time passes all too fast. Our people, who have to suffer from poverty, from life's wear and tear, and the abuses of power, don't have unlimited resources. They can't afford casual conversation. Telling them to wait is the same as telling them to shut up and give in. Purity is the same as compromise. Saying 'but you're still a student, but you're still young,' why, it's just like saying 'grow up first then eat; after you're old wear clothes; found a family first and then sleep.' If we put everything off till tomorrow, we end up caught in tomorrow's snare. And for a girl to be talking politics—because after all, logically speaking, telling people not to get involved in politics is a way of talking politics—for a girl to talk politics, well, I find it ridiculous. Women make a mess of things, then men sort them out. It's as if women know how to produce kids but have no idea how to raise them as human beings. Politics is not a matter of giving birth but of raising, not a matter of making a mess of things but of putting them right, that's what I think. Women should stay out of these problems. If ever I need some knitting done, I'll ask for your advice. We're not knitting socks at present. You think we've gone to the trouble of getting together, the six of us, and coming all this way, just to knit a pair of socks? You'd best get some sleep. We'll go to another room and talk a bit more."

The air had become icy, and the flat-faced student who looked like a farmer tried to lighten the atmosphere with some humor.

"Hyon-Su's right there. We certainly didn't come here to knit socks. We came to swim."

But the student representatives did not laugh.

An hour later, she was on her way back to Rome. Her father had long been urging her to return. During her absence, he had arranged her marriage with prince Livio Savelli. Vanina had scarcely arrived before he spoke of it with her, trembling as he did so. To his great amazement, she consented from the very start. That same evening, in the residence of the countess Vitteleschi, her father presented don Livio to her more or less officially; she spoke with him at length. He was the most elegant youth, with the finest head of hair; at the same time, while he was admitted to have a deal of wit his character was considered so light that he was suspected of nothing by the government authorities. Vanina thought that by first turning his head, she could make of him a very useful agent. Since he was the nephew of Mgr Savelli-Catanzara, governor of Rome and minister in charge of the police, she supposed that spies would never dare to follow him.

After having for several days treated very kindly the amiable don Livio, Vanina informed him that he would never be her husband; in her opinion, he was too light headed.

On the following day, Sa-Mi returned to Seoul. No sooner had she come back than her father began to make a fuss about the question of her marriage. The fact that his daughter had gone to the seaside on her own had provoked him. Sa-Mi's father no longer went poking about in filthy swamps, returning with a catch of tadpoles; he had given that up and was now concentrating all his attention on one single tadpole.

He was less than enchanted at the fact that his major field was not surgery but parasitology, yet there was no one apart from Kim Sok-Hun capable of becoming his son-in-law, fit to inherit that sign-board. It was three days after Sa-Mi's return from the coast that Sok-Hun came ringing at the front door, ever so casually, one long and one short ring. Beyond the shadow of a doubt, Dr. Choi had summoned him.

"Your face is nicely sunburned. You were getting so pale, I thought you must have worms. Lots of people are reluctant to get rid of them. All those fellows who raise parasites in their insides, I mean. So how's Hyon-Su getting on?"

I nearly slapped his face. I had the impression that with his lesson about parasites he was suggesting that Hyon-Su was like a filthy roundworm, sucking my blood inside me.

"Sunburned? Do people get suntanned even in storms then?"

"Oh, of course, there was a storm, wasn't there? Now I look, you're not tanned, after all. Though I know a way of making you get tanned even in a storm. Medically, I mean. Suppose we change the subject?"

"To you, I assume?"

"Not at all; I was thinking about your father. Have you watched him lately while he was operating? You have to have some sense of duty toward your parents, even if you don't love them. Your father's hands have begun to shake; it's what's commonly known as palsy, a fatal symptom for a surgeon: your father can no longer perform major operations. A lot of people think that Choi Ho-Un Surgery is a synonym for what a surgery is, but now the famous doctor can no longer perform operations. You're the loveliest of parasites, Sa-Mi. Do you think that Dr Choi would be so upset at being afflicted with palsy if he wasn't all the time thinking of you? Not at all. It was for you alone that your father sliced and sliced all these years, until now his time is up. It's not so much that he may be going to become my father-in-law; he's my teacher. I can't measure up to a daughter's concern for her father, of course, but I feel a sense of duty, all the same. Marry me. Even if you don't love me. Just do your duty toward your father."

"You may be able to get your hands on the hospital, but you'll never be able to own me. I'll tell you bluntly: I may sometimes have felt sorry for father, and I've never once felt any respect or obligation toward him. A long time ago he amputated my two legs with that great skill of his. I don't have the kind of legs that would allow me to rise, stand and walk on my own. Since that's how helpless I am, I suppose I may end up being married to you. But it'll be like gaining possession of an empty room."

"Gently, there's nothing to get excited about. Surgeons anesthetize patients before they amputate their legs on the operating table. But there's one odd thing. When the patients wake up from the anesthetic, they have absolutely no awareness that their legs have been cut off. Their two legs are still vividly there in their sensation. Even though the legs have been cut off, the sensation of them is still there. In that sensation, the legs are as alive as they were before. It's what Merleau-Ponty christened 'phantom legs.' Everyone's the same. You must think I am vulgar. That's how I see myself and is there any reason why you should think any differently? Wait till you're a bit older, then you'll see. When you're that little bit older, you'll see why clowns can always frolic about on the stage so cheerfully, even when they've nothing to feel happy about. It's all a matter of phantom legs. You're not the only one to have lost your legs. I have too, Dr Choi has too, even Hyon-Su has.... Humans are what you call legless from birth. Only because in our sensation they're still alive, we take our phantom legs for real ones and try to walk and run and move about without a moment's respite. That world of pure love you keep dreaming of, that's nothing more than phantom legs too. If your legs can't run, at least you can hobble with a crutch. It's because I can serve as your crutch that I'm here asking you to marry me. You really are lovely. You must marry me. I have no ideals, so I don't get things wrong. After all, a crutch is just a block of wood."

Sa-Mi kept slowly turning the pages of her text book vacantly. What a shame, the devotion of Vanina for Missirilli. Missirilli was truly detestable. Vanina was truly pitiful. The more pitiful Vanina was and the more she strove to save Missirilli, the more she detested the carbonaro. He looked to her like some kind of buffoon propping himself up with vanity, not like a gallant patriot. As she reached the passage where, in order to have Missirilli back in her arms, Vanina denounces his companions then employs a strategy to remove him from the scene of the arrest, she suddenly began to tremble.

Vanina only emerged from her distraction to say to Pietro:
"Will you spend twenty-four hours with me at the castle of San Nicolo? Your assembly this evening has no need of your presence. Tomorrow morning at San Nicolo, we can walk; that will calm your spirits and give you all the sang-froid you need in such great circumstances."
Pietro consented.
(...)
She went to pay an indispensable visit to the priest in the village of San Nicolo; he was perhaps a spy for the Jesuits. Returning in time for dinner at seven, she found that the little room in which her lover had been hiding was empty. Beside herself, she went running all over the house in search of him; he was nowhere to be found. Desperate, she went back to the little room; only then did she see a note. She read:
"I am going to surrender to the legate; I despair of our cause, the heavens are against us. Who can have betrayed us? Apparently the wretch who threw himself into the well. Since my life is of no use to poor Italy, I would not wish my companions, on seeing that I alone was not arrested, to think that perhaps I had sold them. Farewell. If you love me, take steps to avenge me. Destroy, annihilate the villain who betrayed us, even if it were my own father."

In May the next year, the army staged its revolutionary coup and as martial law was being proclaimed Sa-Mi went to see Hyon-Su for the last time. That was no wind whispering. The

May streets were loud with the sound of decrees being broadcast from radio loudspeakers. Whether it be the government buildings guarded by fully-armed soldiers, or the roads from which traffic had been banned, the posters, the leaflets, or the newspapers with their fine print...the sound was echoing from everything in excited tones an octave higher than usual. If only there had not been that sound, it would have been May as usual, too lovely to be true.... As she emerged from her home, Sa-Mi suddenly found herself wondering what "our motherland" meant. The nation, corruption, starvation, revolution, freedom, public commitments, fulfilling duties, each of these slogans came with a walnut-like shell too hard for her to break with her bare hands. Plane, ailanthus, willow...the names of the Maytime roadside trees now budding, or Shirley MacLaine, Pascale Petit, Orson Wells, Alain Delon, Nathalie Wood, she invoked inwardly the names of various movie actors, each with their own expressions and gestures. Those names did not evoke the same feelings now as a few days before. Sa-Mi could not deny that something was changing. Suddenly a jeep roared past in front of her, sporting a flag. A bundle of pamphlets was scattered from one window. Children were enthusiastically picking up the flying pamphlets. One leaflet, borne on the wind like a leaf, stuck to Sa-Mi's high heel. A child that had come running hoping to pick it up stood now staring up at her face with a disappointed expression. It was still only May, yet the child was wearing a mere singlet.

His face and neck were covered in coal-black dirt, and he had a scratch in his brow clearly inflicted by a finger nail, perhaps in a fight with other kids. The child seemed convinced that Sa-Mi was about to pick up the leaflet. She picked it up and held it out to him, at which he looked embarrassed, hesitated for a moment before suddenly taking the pamphlet, snatching it from her and pursuing the other urchins as they ran into an alley. Sa-

Mi had glimpsed his eyes. Unlike his torn singlet or his dirty face, they were bright and pure. As she met the urchin's gaze, Sa-Mi felt as if she were seeing Hyon-Su. Hyon-Su? Sa-Mi felt that she absolutely had to go and see him in his boarding-house. She had to go and meet Hyon-Su once more; it would be the last time, she promised herself. She reflected that she seemed destined to become Sok-Hun's wife, after all. But still, she wanted to try one last time, just once.

Hyon-Su was staring blankly down at the floor in the dark room, his boarding-house room. Once again, a strange feeling of affection, of familiarity spread through my heart. For the first time I sensed that I was captivated by him, drawn down as if caught in fronds of seaweed. Until that moment I had never once so much as dreamed that he had that power over me.

"What are you doing?"

"Just waiting. They're coming to get me. This is the first time I've ever waited for someone whose name and face I don't know. Of course, they may not come at all."

I had already guessed what was going on. Still I asked, feigning ignorance, "What on earth are you talking about?"

"They've been arrested. It's no great loss if they get caught. They went charging in like kids to pick the summer grapes, draped in old coats like bolsheviks. The new land I'd been dreaming of was not like the land of the past at all; it was a land of abundance lying far far away in the future, a splendid land that no one had ever reached before. But now I think I'm slowly seeing that it was all nothing but hallucinations in a fever."

How happy I was! We embraced again: we must try to find that new land within our little breasts. You were wrong to go looking for it in the outside world. And I comforted him, saying that being young meant being like a child that keeps scraping its knees as it learns to walk, or like a patient, an impetuous patient who keeps falling down when his plaster is removed, finds himself back in plaster again, then falls on his face once more on being released from the plaster.

"But why are you waiting for someone to come? You're safe!"

Then I saw his eyes start to glint again. I told him it was May, that the breeze that had lingered in the gardens before had come back again; it was May, and squirrels were climbing the trunks of trees in the woodlands again, until he made as if to kick the door open and go rushing outside.

"They'll call me a traitor. I can't stand the fact that I alone am breathing the fresh breeze in the Maytime sunlight. I simply watched from the sidelines while they went on with their wrong ideas. It was the end of their youth. I stood there watching with my hands behind my back, watching their youth fixed and wasting in plaster. But someone is sure to come for me as they came for the rest."

"Perhaps no one will come. Why should they? What crime can they accuse you of? Why, you're no criminal, not in the least! When they carried you into the clinic, even with your eyelids all swollen up like that, I looked you straight in the eyes. Your gaze was purer than the sky of May devoid of the slightest trace of dust. Nobody seeing your eyes could ever believe that you might commit a crime."

"Not so; I was the one who first started the group. I was the one who talked to them about a new land, a new hospital. If I hadn't talked to them like that, they would have stayed the kind of fellows able to marry someone like you and go for outings in old palace gardens on Sundays unwrapping toffees for their kids. Of course I saw that they were deviating and ended up leaving the group a month ago, but I was responsible for it all. I can't go telling the investigators that my name on the list of members ought to have been crossed out a month ago. Of course, if I speak like that, I may be safe. But people will say I betrayed my friends in order to save my skin. But it's not misunderstandings I'm afraid of. It's only if I suffer together with them, that I'll really have the chance to help them see that they were on the wrong path, that the new land doesn't lie in that direction. First they have to trust me, then I'll have a chance to tell them the truth!"

"You mean you're going to lie? Why are you determined to destroy yourself by making a false deposition? You want to escape from me, to run away from the flowers and the purity of white snowdrifts you love, by lying. Why are you determined to turn your back on happiness? Are you some kind of Jesus, taking other people's sins upon yourself?"

"Old dirty clothes are more comfortable to wear than new ones, and unhappiness suits me better. I cannot be with them! I must choose the direction of duty: I must love all those sick people who were drawn after that quack doctor, rather than one person's love. Affection is sweet as a spring evening, but it's very brief; while duty is wretchedly cold and long, going on and on though your hands are frozen. I have no choice but to let my youth burn like a bonfire for the sake of that long night. A fire lit in the fields that anyone can approach and enjoy. Let all the cold people come. That fire will continue to blaze so long as any fuel remains. You can come too. You mustn't complain if you're just one among many."

I was no longer listening to him. In my heart I was screaming: "It's a phantom leg. What you call your duty is just one phantom leg. Don't try to run. Don't run. You can't run. We haven't had that leg since the day we were born. Don't try to run with a phantom leg across those rugged plains."

"A phantom leg, you say?"

Professor K stopped on his way down the stairs and looked back.

"Aha, I see you know your Merleau-Ponty!"

Professor K's face was suffused with an expression of pure amazement. As if to say that he alone ought to know such things. It was as if he considered it to be some kind of magic spell that nobody except people erudite like himself should ever know or speak. Or was he putting on an amazed expression deliberately, just to give that impression?

"A phantom leg...yes, that is a term Merleau-Ponty employed in a book named *Phénoménologie de la perception* published in 1945...but it will take some time to explain. So finally, the main point of your question. By the way, what was your name again? Miss Choi Yon-Mi? Miss Choi.... Choi.... Yon-Hee, isn't it? The professor with his wonderful memory, who needed only to hear the words 'phantom leg' to recall the name of Merleau-Ponty, that foreigner with the name so difficult to spell, recalling precisely that the book in question had been published, not in 1944, not in 1946, but in 1945, yet who could not recall my name in the time it took him to go down five steps, told me to come to his office. All that was a blessing for me. Because so long as he did not know my name, there would be no encroachment on my ignorance, my shame, to say nothing of all my secrets, and no need for me to be in his power, he would be someone quite unrelated to me, nothing but an object, a mere encyclopedia....

"Come down to my office. It's an interesting question. To think that there are people with intellectual curiosity even among the girl students. Well..."

So it was that one student, equipped with intellectual curiosity, found herself obliged, all the while regretting acutely ever having asked the question, to follow Professor K down the stairs. In his office, everything was faded, covered in dust, the books had faded to a pale yellow. In this world there is a law of the museum: the more faded something is, the more authority it has. Women may adorn themselves with mink, professors with intellectual curiosity dress themselves up in that law of the museum. How boring! His explanation of the phantom leg was far removed from that I had heard from Kim Sok-Hun.... That picture doesn't match the rigid atmosphere of the room, I wonder who it's by? If it hadn't been for that reproduction entitled *Des toits rouges* (red roofs) I would surely have suffocated. Professor K asked me if I knew the Gestalt theory in psychology. I answered that I had never heard of it but that it sounded a lot like Hitler's secret police, the Gestapo, at which he looked insulted and continued in his harsh voice with a lecture which had neither beginning nor end, in which psychology and philosophy, to say nothing of grammar and literature, were all combined, until the sun was setting, the last rays of sunlight were shining on the roof of the university chapel, and cleaners, wearing white masks like those worn by doctors in the operating room, began to sweep the corridors, the empty expanses of empty corridor.

"So now do you see what it's about? He wanted to prove by means of the experience people have of phantom legs that the human nervous system, the human body is no mere mechanism. Put briefly, he was refuting mechanistic psychology. The world's not there just because it's there. It's there because I make it be there. Because there is a resolve and inclination to that effect, people feel that they have legs even when they have lost them. It's not a matter of the leg being there and we feeling it; because we have the sensation that the leg is there, it is there. Therefore we can see that a human leg is fundamentally different from the accessories of some kind of machine. If we follow this theory we arrive as he does at the conclusion that the human person is 'condemned to sense.'

Only think of the relationship that exists between words and a sentence, for instance!"

"But I detest grammar. I believe that each individual word matters, every single word, simply rolling like a stone across a plain freely provoking our unbounded imagination. That's different from words with their meanings constrained in grammar, unable to budge an inch, bound together with other words inside sentences, in grammatical constructions...there's a sound of chains in grammar and sentences."

Then I went on to say that the irregular verbs in French, those of the third declension, afforded us far more relief than the regularly declining verbs of the first and second declensions. Professor K had picked up an envelope, one addressed to him, bearing the name of a government agency, and stood up after slipping a few note books into the envelope.

"My explanation seems to have been insufficient. Just remember this. In theory a rose and its crimson hue can be separated but our experience tells us that it is impossible for us to perceive them apart. The same is true of the relationship between the words and a phrase, the relationship between us and reality...to say nothing of the relationship between mind and body, for the meaning of the part is determined by an understanding of the whole. Besides, the human mind is no passive machine like a slot-machine that begins to move when you insert a coin; the mind functions in accordance with a fundamental desire for some kind of form...those are not my own words, mark you...so any way, the notion of 'phantom legs' teaches us a new sense of humanity. It means that even if a leg with its meaning is amputated, we still don't lose it."

I stood watching Professor K go out through the gate of the university. His form seen from behind...and even after he had completely disappeared beyond the gate, his shadow lingered behind for a while and I saw it flutter briefly outside the gateway.

Ah! wasn't that his "phantom leg" whose shadow was lingering and fluttering although he himself had completely vanished?

Sa-Mi was turning the final pages of her French text book, *Vanina Vanini*. In her heart, the last meeting of Vanini with Missirilli, and her own last meeting with Hyon-Su accompanied each other in double relief. In the background stretched a murky sky into which rose the prison's grim chimney.

At last the day dawned that was to determine Vanina's fate. Early in the morning, she withdrew into the prison chapel. Who could ever tell what thoughts troubled her all through the long day? Did Missirilli love her enough to pardon her? She had denounced his companions, but she had saved his life. Once reason had triumphed in that tormented soul, Vanina hoped he would consent to leave Italy with her: if she had sinned, it was from excess of love. As the hour of four struck, she heard from afar, echoing on the cobbles, the sound of the police horses' hooves. Every single step seemed to pierce her heart. Soon she could make out the rumbling of the carts transporting the prisoners. They stopped in the little square in front of the prison; she saw two officers pull Missirilli to his feet; he was alone in one cart and so loaded with chains that he could not move. "At least he's alive!" she thought, and tears came to her eyes, "they haven't poisoned him yet!" The evening was cruel; the altar lamp, which hung at a great height and for which the jail-keeper was reluctant to use much oil, was the only source of light in the dark chapel. Vanina's eyes wandered over the tombs of various great lords of the Middle Ages, who had died in the adjacent prison. Their statues looked threatening.

All noise had long since ceased; Vanina was absorbed in her black thoughts. A little after midnight had struck, she seemed to hear a slight sound like the wings of a bat. She tried to walk, but fell half-fainting across the altar-rails. At that very moment, two phantoms materialized beside her; she had not heard them approach. She saw the jailer, and Missirilli so laden with chains that he seemed to be swathed in them. The jailer opened a dark lantern, that he perched on the balustrade before the altar in such a way that he could clearly see his prisoner. After which he withdrew to the back, near the door. He had scarcely moved away before Vanina hurled herself at Missirilli's neck. As she hugged him she could feel nothing but his cold, sharp chains. "Who gave him these chains?" she wondered. She felt no pleasure in embracing her love. That pain was followed by another yet more poignant; Missirilli's welcome was so cold that for a moment she believed that he knew what she had done.

At last he spoke: "Dear friend, I regret the love you have come to feel for me. I seek in vain to find what merit may have inspired it in you. Believe me, we should return to more Christian sentiments, forget the illusion that once led us astray; I cannot be yours. Who knows, the constant misfortune that has dogged my undertakings may perhaps come from the state of mortal sin in which I have constantly lived. Even if I only listen to the counsels of human prudence, why was I not arrested with my friends, that fatal night in Forli? Why, at the moment of danger, was I not at my post? Why has my absence there given rise to the cruelest suspicions? Because I had a passion other than the freedom of Italy."

Vanina could not recover from the astonishment caused by the change in Missirilli. He had not perceptibly lost weight, yet he looked thirty. Vanina attributed the change in him to the bad treatment he had suffered in prison, and dissolved into tears.

"Ah! The jailers swore they would treat you kindly."

The fact of the matter is that, with death near at hand, all the religious principles that might accord with a passion for the freedom of Italy had reawakened in the young carbonero's heart. Gradually Vanina perceived that the amazing change she had noted in her lover was entirely moral, not at all the effect of physical ill-treatment. Her pain, that she had believed already complete, grew yet more intense.

Missirilli stood silent; Vanina seemed on the verge of suffocating with sobbing. He added, looking slightly moved himself:

"If I were to love anything on this earth, Vanina, it would be you; but praise God, I have no longer any goal in life other than to die, either in prison, or striving to bring freedom to Italy."

Again there was silence; clearly, Vanina could not speak, she tried in vain. Missirilli added:

"Duty is cruel, my dear; but if it did not cost a little suffering to fulfill it, where would be the heroism? Give me your word that you will never again attempt to see me."

In so far as the tightness of his chain allowed it, he made a slight movement with his wrist and extended his fingers toward Vanina.

"If you will allow a man who was dear to you to give you advice, marry quietly the meritorious man to whom your father destines you. Confide nothing disturbing to him; but on the other hand, never try to see me again. We must henceforth be as strangers to one another. You have advanced a considerable sum for the good of the nation;

if ever it is delivered from the tyrants, that sum will be faithfully repaid in national goods."

Vanina was thunderstruck. As he addressed her, Pietro's eye had only once glinted, at the moment when he named the nation.

In the end, her pride came to the help of the young princess. She had come with a stock of diamonds and some small files. She replied nothing to Missirilli, but simply offered them to him.

"I accept out of duty, for I must try to escape; but I will never see you again, I swear it here before your new gifts. Adieu, Vanina; promise you will never write to me, never try to see me; let me belong entirely to the nation, I am dead for you: adieu."

"No!" Vanina replied in fury, "I want you to know what I did, led by the love I have for you."

She proceeded to tell him all she had undertaken, from the moment Missirilli had left the castle of San Nicolo to surrender to the legate. Once she had finished that tale, she continued:

"Yet all that is nothing: I have done more, in love for you."

Then she told him of her betrayal.

"Ah! monster," Pietro exclaimed in fury; throwing himself on her, he tried to strike her down with his chains.

He would have succeeded had it not been for the jailer, who came running at the first shouts. He seized Missirilli.

"Here, monster, I will owe you nothing," said Missirilli to Vanina, throwing in her face, in so far as the chains allowed it, the files and diamonds; then he moved rapidly away.

Vanina stood there, appalled. She returned to Rome. Now the papers announce that she has just wed prince don Livio Savelli.

It must have been about a month after Hyon-Su went to prison, that Sa-Mi skipped class in order to visit him. In the prison visiting-room, Sa-Mi sat waiting for her number to be called, repeating to herself that she was not going to cry. Her waiting here was pointless. What difference could meeting him possibly make?

In his prison uniform, Hyon-Su looked like someone different. I had come to make one last effort, or scene, to prevent him from testifying against himself in court and I set out to do just that, holding back by tears and clenching my fists.

How could I help crying, though, when I saw him, all haggard in his baggy uniform? On seeing me, Hyon-Su forced himself to smile but a shadow of pain, like that I used to see when the dressings were removed from his wounds, immediately swallowed up the smile.

"Tell the truth. Your friends are trying to put all the blame on you in the hope of saving their own skins. Tell the truth. Just tell the truth. You're still young, aren't you? There's still time for you to break another leg. Father's cough gets worse and worse as the days go by. He hopes that before he dies I'll get married to the boy I detest most in the world. Look, he's already sent me the ring."

I pulled the ring from my bag and tried to give it to Hyon-Su, but the warden present at the interview stopped me. Supposing I'd given it to him, he'd surely have hurled it back.

"Sa-Mi, our time is almost up. There's only three minutes left of the time allowed us. I ought to condense all the things I might have said over a whole lifetime into these three minutes, but nothing comes to mind. I can only promise you this: I tried with all my might to find the new land I'm dreaming of in your room, that quiet room where if you open the window you can look down into the garden full of geraniums and other flowers blooming. Only the land I'm dreaming of is not that small. I still believe in it, you know. If the devil carried you off, I would lament and cry, but I wouldn't give up my youth for you. One thing more: I told you I hated flowers and snow, didn't I? Not at all, not at all, absolutely not. It's on account of those flowers and those snowflakes, on account of things like them that are helpless because they're pure, that I stretched out both hands toward the icy winter. May's revolution has only just begun and I have no idea at all how it will end. But you will have your house with the pretty Dutch-style roof, completely untouched by all those things. You'll be able to find satisfaction in your children, even when they're a bit too playful. Good times will come, for sure. One day I'll go to see your garden, where it's forever and ever May. I'll go to see the Maytime plants that will never grow any darker green than they are now, where the shoots will never grow any longer than they are now. Goodbye, our time's up. I'd like to congratulate you on your wedding day, but you know that I can't be there. Look at me. That pure look of yours gave me a lot of courage. But that's the reason why I've deliberately been telling myself that you're the real traitor. Now I realize that it's simply not true at all. If it weren't for you, if it weren't for your eyes looking down at me from that upstairs room with its sixty watt bulb burning, I would have ended up plunging either into the sewers of power or into the clouds of cheapskate heroics. Goodbye. The time's up."

Day was dawning bright. Sa-Mi noted that the noise from the trams was little by little becoming more distinct while the houses and the trees on the hillsides, that had lost all form, were slowly beginning to return to the light. The sound of her father's coughing rose with increasing strength from downstairs.

"Deprived of sound and light, we're as good as dead. I know that it's wrong to attempt to preserve any one sound and light. Sound and light are not reality. Now I realize that it's the other way round. If there is no sound, the bell might as well not exist; if there's no light, the mirror held in our palm no matter how firmly might just as well not be there. What I glimpsed for the last time when I was twenty was the sound and light of everything."

Day is breaking. Today the last exam will be over. She reflected that until now she had delayed, pleading the excuse that she would marry Sok-Hun only after she had graduated from university; but once this exam was past, she would no longer have that excuse. She closed the book and murmured in a low voice, "I wonder if I can get an A on *Vanina Vanini*?"

Professor K closed the book and shouted, "*C'est fini*. It's all done." Then he continued, "Once you've graduated, you'll be in a hurry to get married like Vanina. But if we meet in the street, don't shudder for fear your husband will be jealous. Say hello, will you?"

"*C'est fini!*"

Professor K rubbed the chalk from his hands as he waited for the students to laugh.

Modern Fiction from Korea

Father and Son: A Novel by Han Sung-won
Translated by Yu Young-nan & Julie Pickering
ISBN: 1-931907-04-8, Paperback, $17.95

An age-old struggle between the generations of modern industrialization and the battle for democratic freedoms in Korea. The author explores the role of the intellectual in modern Korean society and the changing face of the Korean family.

Reflections on a Mask: Two Novellas by Ch'oe In-hun
Translated by Stephen Moore & Shi C. P. Moore
ISBN: 1-931907-05-6, Paperback, $16.95

Reflections on a Mask explores the disillusionment and search for identity of a young man in the post-Korean War era. *Christmas Carol* uses the themes of hope and salvation to examine relationships within a patriarchal Korean family.

Unspoken Voices: Selected Short Stories by Korean Women Writers
Compiled and Translated by Jin-Young Choi, Ph.D.
ISBN: 1-931907-06-4, Paperback, $16.95

Stories by twelve Korean women writers whose writings penetrate into the lives of Korean women from the early part of the 20th century to the present. Writers included are: Choi Junghee, Han Musook, Kang Shinjae, Park Kyongni, Lee Sukbong, Lee Jungho, Song Wonhee, Park Wansuh, Yoon Jungsun, Un Heekyong, Kong Jeeyoung and Han Kang.

The General's Beard: Two Novellas by Lee Oyoung
Translated by Brother Anthony
ISBN: 1-931907-07-2, Paperback, $14.95

In *The General's Beard*, a journalist tries to solve the mystery of a young photographer's death. In *Phantom Legs*, a young girl studying French literature meets a student wounded during demonstrations and begins an ambiguous relationship with him.

Farmers: A Novel by Lee Mu-young
Translated by Yu Young-nan
ISBN: 1-931907-08-0, Paperback, $15.95

The novel is about Korea's Tonghak Uprising the 1894. A farmer-turned Tonghak leader who left the village several years ago in the wake of a severe flogging returns to his village to take revenge of his exploiters.

More titles from Homa & Sekey Books

Flower Terror: Suffocating Stories of China by Pu Ning
ISBN 0-9665421-0-X, Fiction, Paperback, $13.95

"The stories in this work are well written." – Library Journal

Acclaimed Chinese writer eloquently describes the oppression of intellectuals in his country between 1950s and 1970s in these twelve autobiographical novellas and short stories. Many of the stories are so shocking and heart-wrenching that one cannot but feel suffocated.

The Peony Pavilion: A Novel by Xiaoping Yen, Ph.D.
ISBN 0-9665421-2-6, Fiction, Paperback, $16.95

"A window into the Chinese literary imagination." – Publishers Weekly

A sixteen-year-old girl visits a forbidden garden and falls in love with a young man she meets in a dream. She has an affair with her dream-lover and dies longing for him. After her death, her unflagging spirit continues to wait for her dream-lover. Does her lover really exist? Can a youthful love born of a garden dream ever blossom? The novel is based on a sixteenth-century Chinese opera written by Tang Xianzu, "the Shakespeare of China."

Butterfly Lovers: A Tale of the Chinese Romeo and Juliet
by Fan Dai, Ph.D., ISBN 0-9665421-4-2, Fiction, Paperback, $16.95

"An engaging, compelling, deeply moving, highly recommended and rewarding novel." – Midwest Books Review

A beautiful girl disguises herself as a man and lives under one roof with a young male scholar for three years without revealing her true identity. They become sworn brothers, soul mates and lovers. In a world in which marriage is determined by social status and arranged by parents, what is their inescapable fate?

The Dream of the Red Chamber: An Allegory of Love
By Jeannie Jinsheng Yi, Ph.D., ISBN: 0-9665421-7-7, Hardcover
Asian Studies/Literary Criticism, $49.95

Although dreams have been studied in great depth about this most influential classic Chinese fiction, the study of all the dreams as a sequence and in relation to their structural functions in the allegory is undertaken here for the first time.

More titles from Homa & Sekey Books

Always Bright: Paintings by American Chinese Artists 1970-1999
Edited by Xue Jian Xin et al.
ISBN 0-9665421-3-4, Art, Hardcover, $49.95

"An important, groundbreaking, seminal work." – Midwest Book Review

A selection of paintings by eighty acclaimed American Chinese artists in the late 20th century, *Always Bright* is the first of its kind in English publication. The album falls into three categories: oil painting, Chinese painting and other media painting. It also offers profiles of the artists and information on their professional accomplishment.

Always Bright, Vol. II: Paintings by Chinese American Artists
Edited by Eugene Wang, Ph.D., et al.
ISBN: 0-9665421-6-9, Art, Hardcover, $50.00

A sequel to the above, the book includes artworks of ninety-two artists in oil painting, Chinese painting, watercolor painting, and other media such as mixed media, acrylic, pastel, pen and pencil, etc. The book also provides information on the artists and their professional accomplishment. Artists included come from different backgrounds, use different media and belong to different schools. Some of them enjoy international fame while others are enterprising young men and women who are more impressionable to novelty and singularity.

Dai Yunhui's Sketches by Dai Yunhui
ISBN: 1-931907-00-5, Art, Paperback, $14.95

Over 50 sketches from an artist of attainment who is especially good at sketching stage and dynamic figures. His drawings not only accurately capture the dynamic movements of the performers, but also acutely catch the spirit of the stage artists.

Musical Qigong: Ancient Chinese Healing Art from a Modern Master
By Shen Wu, ISBN: 0-9665421-5-0, Health, Paperback, $14.95

Musical Qigong is a special healing energy therapy that combines two ancient Chinese traditions-healing music and Qigong. This guide contains two complete sets of exercises with photo illustrations and discusses how musical Qigong is related to the five elements in the ancient Chinese concept of the universe - metal, wood, water, fire, and earth.

More titles from Homa & Sekey Books

Ink Paintings by Gao Xingjian, Nobel Prize Winner
ISBN: 0-931907-03-X, Hardcover, Art, $34.95

An extraordinary art book by the Nobel Prize Winner for Literature in 2000, this volume brings together over sixty ink paintings by Gao Xingjian that are characteristic of his philosophy and painting style. Gao believes that the world cannot be explained, and the images in his paintings reveal the black-and-white inner world that underlies the complexity of human existence. People admire his meditative images and evocative atmosphere by which Gao intends his viewers to visualize the human conditions in extremity.

Splendor of Tibet: The Potala Palace, Jewel of the Himalayas
By Phuntsok Namgyal
ISBN: 1-931907-02-1, Hardcover, Art/Architecture, $39.95

A magnificent and spectacular photographic book about the Potala Palace, the palace of the Dalai Lamas and the world's highest and largest castle palace. Over 150 rare and extraordinary color photographs of the Potala Palace are showcased in the book, including murals, thang-ka paintings, stupa-tombs of the Dalai Lamas, Buddhist statues and scriptures, porcelain vessels, enamel work, jade ware, brocade, Dalai Lamas' seals, and palace exteriors.

The Haier Way: The Making of a Chinese Business Leader and a Global Brand by Jeannie J. Yi, Ph.D., & Shawn X. Ye, MBA
ISBN: 1-931907-01-3, Hardcover, Business, $24.95

Haier is the largest consumer appliance maker in China. The book traces the appliance giant's path to success, from its early bleak years to its glamorous achievement when Haier was placed the 6th on Forbes Global's worldwide household appliance manufacturer list in 2001. The book explains how Haier excelled in quality, service, technology innovation, a global vision and a management style that is a blend of Jack Welch of "GE" and Confucius of ancient China.

www.homabooks.com

Order Information: U.S.: $4.00 for the first item, $1.50 for each additional item. **Outside U.S.:** $10.00 for the first item, $5.00 for each additional item. Please send a check or money order in U.S. fund (payable to Homa & Sekey Books) to: Orders Department, Homa & Sekey Books, P.O. Box 103, Dumont, NJ 07628 U.S.A. Tel: 201-384-6692; Fax: 201-384-6055; Email: info@homabooks.com